THE MORTICIAN AND THE CLOWN

BOOK THREE OF A JULIA LILLUS SERIES

JAMES ROBERTS

Edited by
JAMES ROBERTS
Illustrated by
JAMES ROBERTS

❀ Created with Vellum

For those who have become victims of sexual assault.

For all of the children and young adults who have been taken from us and exploited beyond belief; this book is a reminder to us all, how cruel our society has become so we can, together, end such tragedies.

CONTENTS

INTRODUCTION

"The Mortician And The Clown" is the Third Book Of A Julia Lillus Series and is a culmination of experiences intertwined with romantic relationships, erotic sex, and rape beyond comprehension.

The book depicts character personalities, good and bad, underlining conflicts and their resolution; dark secrets of rape and human exploitation; exploring the pain and devastation it causes.

The reader will experience anger, disappointment, exasperation, vulnerability, and joy; discover the resolution to each of these emotions with a feeling of satisfaction with hope in the future.

This book continues a Series of Books One and Two; introducing new adventures while introducing new characters.

CHARACTERS - JOHN DICKERSON

John Dickerson is a recent college graduate in the studies of Mortuary Sciences.

John Dickerson is a newcomer to the Community of Harford and strives to set up his business to be the number one Mortuary and in the surrounding area.

CHARACTERS - JOSEPH LINDSEY

Joseph Lindsey is a convict at the Jackson City Prison. His convictions are for rape and murder.

Joseph finished his time and is being released from the prison.

It is not clear whether he has learned from his convictions and it is questionable how he will function in society.

CHARACTERS - LAURIE LIBBY

Laurie Libby is a young twenty-eight year old beautiful female newcomer to the Cloverville Community.

She works as a court stenographer and is considered a 'proper lady' in her feminine mannerisms.

CHARACTERS - JUDD FINNEY

Judd Finney is a thirty year old male who hires as a clown. His specialty is showing as a clown in children's hospitals and community parks.

Judd Finney is a newcomer to the Harford Community.

CHARACTERS - JULIA LILLUS

Julia Lillus is the Chief of Police for the Harford Community. She has
been with the Department for several years and has a keen sense of
knowing when things 'just don't add up.'

Julia is in her early thirties and has recently lost her husband in an
unfortunate incident.

CHARACTERS - RICHARD PELTZ

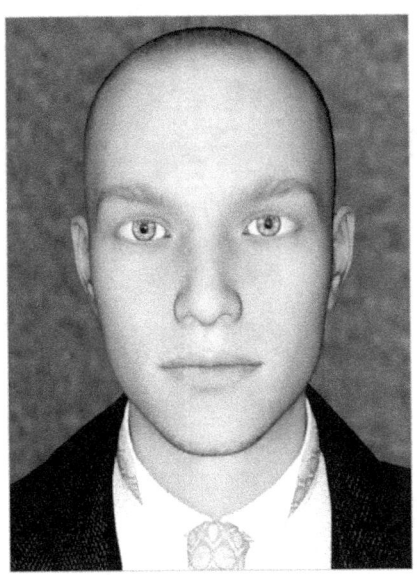

Richard Peltz is a Deputy Officer for the Harford Police Department and has worked in that capacity for several years.

At thirty years old, he feels it is time to settle down with a wife and start a family.

CHARACTERS - BOBBIE PELTZ

Bobbie Peltz is a young and beautiful woman in her mid twenties and has found the love of her life with Richard Peltz.

Bobbie is the newest Deputy Officer for the Harford Police Department. She has a gift of being able to counsel in family and child situations and disputes.

CHARACTERS - AMANDA ALEXANDRIA

Amanda Alexandria is a twenty-five year old Forensics Specialist whose hometown is downstate in New York City. She is moving to the Community of Harford to take a job with the Harford Police Department functioning in her expertise.

A Forensics Lab has been a needed addition to the Department.

CHARACTERS - CINDY MYERS

Cindy Myers is an eleven year old girl who frequents the Harford Community Park and becomes intrigued by the clown who has come to the community.

CHARACTERS - KAITLIN BAKER

Kaitlin Baker is a fourteen year old girl who becomes acquainted with Cindy Myers in a peculiar fashion.

CHARACTERS - MARY FINNEGAN

Mary Finnegan is a thirteen year old girl who becomes acquainted with Cindy, Kaitlin, and Claire.

CHARACTERS - CLAIRE LAWSON

Claire Lawson is a girl of thirteen who becomes acquainted with Cindy, Mary, and Kaitlin.

PREFACE

James Roberts

John Dickerson, a recent graduate of the studies for Mortuary Sciences, settles in the Harford Community.

John's motives are questionable and Chief Julia Lillus becomes skeptical.

He pairs with an ex-convict in sinister activities.

John's newly wedded wife discovers something that pushes her beyond comprehension.

A clown comes to the Harford Community and takes up residence. He hangs out in Children's Hospitals and the Community Park.

Within the Harford Community, sinister events start to unfold leading to a nightmare beyond belief.

JOHNNY DICKERSON - ELEMENTARY SCHOOL

J ohnny Dickerson cannot keep his hands to himself and pesters the girls in his classroom.

"Johnny, what are you doing back there?" asks Miss Dummel.

"Nothing," says Johnny.

"He is lying Miss Dummel. He is trying to reach under Lucy's skirt!" exclaims Sara.

"Johnny, keep your hands to yourself. Now, go sit in the corner!" orders Miss Dummel.

"Miss Dummel, while we were at recess today, Johnny Dickerson kept pinching my bottom while I was on the swings. He kept putting his hands under my skirt to do it," says Linda.

"Johnny Dickerson, I want to see you after class today," says Miss Dummel.

"Johnny, some of the girls in class tell me you are touching them in private areas under their dresses."

"Miss Dummel, those girls are lying."

"Johnny, I do not think the girls are lying. I am going to take you to the principal's office."

JOHNNY DICKERSON - MIDDLE SCHOOL

John Dickerson starts to take a different approach to the young females in his school.

"Hey, Johnny Dickerson, I hear you want to talk to me?" asks Lucy.

"Look, Lucy, I do not want you to call me 'Johnny'. We are in middle school, now, and my name is John."

"OK John, sorry! What do you want to talk to me about?"

"Are you going to the field trip, Friday?"

"Yes, I am."

"I would like to sit with you on the bus."

"Sure, John, but you will have to behave yourself," stresses Lucy.

"Lucy, I always behave myself!"

"John, it is not what I hear from the other girls."

"The other girls don't know what they are talking about. They are just jealous because I haven't asked them out for a date."

FRIDAY COMES AND JOHN IS ABOUT TO GET ON THE BUS WITH LUCY TO GO ON THE FIELD TRIP

"Let's go to the back of the bus," says John.

"OK," says Lucy.

"Lucy, I like you, and I would like to make out with you."

"John Dickerson! I told you I would sit with you providing you behaved."

"Can I put my arm around you, Lucy?"

"Well, OK, but I am warning you!"

"John, please take your hand away from my blouse..ouch, John! You pinched my breasts!"

"Oh sorry, my hand slipped, but your breasts do feel real nice."

"John, take your hand out from under my skirt and off my thigh!"

"Lucy, don't be so touchy! It's just a little 'petting'. There can't be much harm in that."

"I am not interested in your 'petting'! I am moving from this seat, John Dickerson!"

JOHNNY DICKERSON - JUNIOR HIGH SCHOOL

J ohn steals a kiss and tries to use his charm in seducing a young female classmate.

"Hey, Linda, can I walk with you to your class? Can I carry your books for you?" asks John.

"OK, if you want to," says Linda.

"So, Linda, how do you like being in Junior High?"

"It's OK, I guess."

"Quick, over here and lean back against the wall. Now close your eyes," says John.

"John, oh, what was that?"

"They call it a 'French Kiss'."

"You better not do that again!"

"Linda, I will not 'beat-around-the-bush'. I want to make out with you."

"What do you have in mind, John?"

"You know, I want to see what is under those clothes of yours and then…!" exclaims John.

"Oh no you won't, John Dickerson! You will need to find another girl for that! Now leave me alone and give me my books!"

JOHN DICKERSON - HIGH SCHOOL

J ohn is trying to get a date for the prom, but he is turned down
because of his reputation in school.

"So, Laura, will you be my date for the senior prom?" asks John.

"I don't know, John. You have quite the reputation around here at
school," answers Laura.

"Reputation? How? What?"

"Come on, John! You can't keep your hands to yourself, and you
want to fuck every girl you see!"

"Laura, I happen to have more of those male hormones than most.
I promise I won't lay a hand on you Laura, even if you are the most
beautiful girl in our class."

"John, flattery will get you nowhere with this girl. I will take a
rain-check on your invitation, John."

"Come-on, Laura! I wouldn't do anything you didn't want. Besides,
we would be in a crowd of classmates. What can happen?"

"No, John!"

JOHN MOVES ON AND FINDS ANOTHER GIRL TO ASK OUT TO THE PROM

"Leslie, will you be my date for the senior prom?" asks John.

"Sure, I'd love to, John, but I won't go for any of your 'out-of-bounds' intimate gestures," says Leslie.

"What do you mean by that, Leslie?"

"I mean, to put it bluntly, I won't fuck you!"

"OK, OK! I will try to behave."

"John I am warning you!"

"OK, please be my date?"

PROM NIGHT

J ohn has figured it is time to make out with a female he finds at
the prom.

"John! Where are we going?" asks Jennifer.

"Just a little ride to get away from all of this," answers John.

"But, you came here with Leslie."

"She is boring. Besides, I like being with you anyway."

"So, where are we going, John?"

"Oh, just to the bluffs, the sunset is amazing," answers John.

JOHN AND JENNIFER ARRIVE AT THE BLUFFS

"John, I think we should not be doing this here."

"Come on Jennifer, what's wrong with a little 'necking' on such a beautiful evening while watching the sunset?"

"I can see why you think Leslie is such a bore. She wouldn't come out here with you, would she?"

"Let's not talk about Leslie. Let's talk about you and me."

"John, I am a proper girl, and I do not want you to think of me as anything different."

"Proper girls need love, too," says John.

"John, please don't do that!"

"Jennifer, you are going to love it! I will be gentle."

"No John, please don't pull my panties off and don't touch me there and no…!"

"There, quiet down. Just spread those legs a little wider," says John.

CLAIRE BETHANY SCHOOL OF MORTUARY SCIENCES

T he Lab, teaching the subject of Rigor Mortis, is about to begin at the college.

"OK class, today we are going to explore the fundamentals of Rigor Mortis and its interaction with the non-living body. Rigor Mortis, the stiffening of body joints, will begin within one to seven hours after death and can be accelerated with temperature changes in the environment around the body. The warmer the body, the slower Rigor Mortis begins. So, it is imperative that you, the mortician, work rather quickly making the body presentable for family calling hours. Do not embalm the body right away due to the procedure instantly triggering Rigor Mortis. Rigor Mortis is first seen within the face; specifically the eyelids, so you will want to close them as soon as possible. If you need more time to work on the body, you will benefit by keeping the body at a warmer temperature. You are to be professional at all times while processing the dead for viewing."

"John, what broad are you going to try to seduce, tonight, after this lab is over?" asks Trevor.

"I don't know. I am running out of prospects!"

"Do you ever think your strategy needs to change? Your approach to a female shouldn't be 'I want to fuck you now' as an ice breaker to getting to know her on a first date," says Trevor.

"Look, Trevor, I don't 'beat around the bush'. I need to get off just about every day."

"Are you sure you are OK? Have you been to see a doctor?"

"I am normal, Trevor! Are you trying to tell me you don't want to get 'laid'?"

"Certainly I do, John, but I don't ask for it on first meeting her or even the first date. Maybe you should take a rest and ask out one of those corpses we have in the labs."

"Now you are being funny Trevor, really funny!"

"Seriously, John, you cannot force sex on those ladies! You will be in jail for rape!"

"I manage to talk them into it! Now, enough chat. I going to get ready for my next date," says John.

MORAVIA STATE INSTITUTE OF THE MENTALLY INSANE

S hortly after graduating from the Claire Bethany School Of Mortuary Sciences John Dickerson is admitted to a Mental Institute for his Immense Sexual Desire Disorder.

"Nurse Jameson, we have a classic case of Necrophilia, here, with our newest patient. He has been begging the orderly to visit the morgue in the basement," says Doctor Faust.

"Doctor, I have noticed he is suffering from Intense Sexual Chemistry to the point of masturbating daily. I have also heard the orderly has had to restrain him from some of the young females we have here. It isn't unusual to see him pushing a female patient on the cafeteria table and trying to get between her legs with his penis sticking out of his pants," says nurse Jameson.

"I am going to sit down with him next week to try to ferret out what is going on in his head and why," says Doctor Faust.

"What should we do with him until the time you talk to him?" asks nurse Jameson.

"Limit his time with the mixed company and keep an eye on him.

The last thing we need is a rape of one of our female patients," says Doctor Faust.

"John, I have called you into my office, so we can have a conversation to what is going on with your thinking. How old are you, John?" asks Doctor Faust.

"I am eighteen years old. I don't think there is anything wrong with me," says John.

"John, you seem to have an unusual intensity for sexual activity. We have noted your masturbation efforts and more importantly, your desire to have sexual intercourse with some of our young female patients."

"I am the typical male! I have trouble getting a date, and I need to release myself just as any male. If I can't get a female to fuck, I have to masturbate, although I don't like to masturbate because there is nothing more satisfying as feeling a pussy wrapped around my cock."

"OK, John, I would like to discuss with you the earlier years in your life. What were your earlier years like in context to your sexual desires?"

"I always wanted to reach under some of my classmate's skirts."

"Why was that, John?"

"I wanted to see pussy and hoping to touch it."

"Were you ever successful with that?"

"No, I was stopped either by the teacher or by the girl."

"So, you stopped because the girl didn't want you to feel her under her dress?"

"Well, the intrigue of discovery faded fast as soon as she knew what I was up to."

"I see, John. How was it when you became a teenager in school?"

"My feelings intensified, and I wasn't 'turned off' if a female student knew I was after her pussy. I never got anywhere with them because I couldn't get them alone."

"What, John, would have happened if you could had gotten the female classmate alone?"

"I would have fucked her!"

"John were you successful in getting any dates?"

"Yeah, I had some dates, but was turned down when I wanted sex, and there were some girls I couldn't get a date because of my reputation."

"What reputation was that, John?"

"The girls learned all I wanted was to fuck them, so they never accepted my invitation for a date."

"How did the girls know this?"

"I asked them to fuck as soon as I met them. I had to; my intense desire was driving me crazy! I had to shoot my load all of the time. Hell, there were times when I masturbated so much, I had no load to shoot, and then my balls ached."

"John, I would like to back up a little and talk about your very early years, say when you were in kindergarten. How was family life, then?"

"It was great! My mom loved me. If I wanted to sleep in her bed with her, she would let me."

"How did your mother react to you when you wanted to sleep in her bed with her?"

"I can remember my mom would give me massages. I loved those, and they felt so good."

"John, how did your mom massage you?"

"She would rub my head and my back. She ran her hands down my legs..."

"How did she rub your legs, John? Did she rub the inner part of your legs or the outer parts of your legs?"

"She would always rub the inner part of my legs. The back of her hands would touch my cock now and then."

"How did that feel, John and did you like it?"

"Every time she touched it with the back of her hands, I would feel a slight twinge, and it would move on its own. If felt good and I had wished she would touch me more."

"Did anything change as you grew older?"

"I continued to sleep in mom's bed whenever she wanted me to."

"Oh, she started asking you to sleep with her in her bed?"

"Yes, and I can remember when she made me 'cum.'"

"Explain what happened, John."

"One night when she was rubbing my legs, she turned her hands over and grasped my cock. I was stunned and confused what was happening to me. I can remember that my cock suddenly swelled and straightened out. It felt good. She started massaging my cock by grasping it in her hand and rubbing it up and down. I remember I was scared because all of a sudden, I felt like I was going to pee in her hand. It felt so good, and before I knew it, I peed in her hand and on the bed."

"John, you knew it wasn't pee, didn't you?"

"At the time, I wasn't sure, but I saw that it was gooey and white. Nothing like pee."

"John, how long did this go on?"

"Mom had me in bed with her at least two to three times a week. When I wasn't in bed with her, I was masturbating in my bed because I had found a new feeling that felt so good."

"John, I know this may be difficult, but you say you would rather have sexual intercourse with female vaginal penetration than masturbating with your hand. How do you know what vaginal penetration feels like? Did it happen at some point in your life? You say you haven't been able to get a date, so I assume there was no vaginal penetration."

"I was in seventh or eighth grade; one night when my mother asked me to her bed, she did her ritual hand massage of my cock until I was stiff. She asked me to kiss her, so the most natural thing for me to be able to do that was to move up over the top of her to kiss her on the cheek. I suddenly felt a feeling with my cock different from the usual massages. She put her arms around me and started moving her hips. I noticed she had both of her hands on my hips and I was wondering how she was still massaging my cock without her hands. I tried to move away from her, but she wouldn't let me go. I felt like I had to pee, again. And, again, it felt so good. I peed just like I did before. Mom finally let her hands off of me, and I was able to move. What I saw, then, was the scariest thing. My cock was sliding out of a hole she had between her legs, and that gooey white stuff was running out of that hole. At that time, I had no idea that I had sexual intercourse with my mother."

"Did this continue with your mother?"

"Yes, she told me what I was doing showed her how much I loved her and that by letting me do it to her, how much she loved me. I learned that by fucking my mother felt so much better than my hand, so I didn't think anything different and continued with her."

"John, the picture you have painted, here, leads me to believe you felt vaginal penetration was a sign of love, most importantly to feed your self-esteem to give you the feeling that someone, your mother in this case, accepted and loved you because of your actions of what you were doing to her and acceptance because she was asking you to do it to her. At that young age, you recognized the difference in feeling vaginal penetration vs. hand masturbating, and that feeling was so good that you did not want to stop and go back to masturbation. So, when your mother stopped having intercourse with you, it is then that you needed to replace what you had with her, so you tried to get dates with various females. The more you were turned down; the more intense your desire became because you desperately needed to get that feeling back to feel accepted and loved. You also did not want to go back to masturbating. Another issue we have here is what is called Necrophilia. It is the desire to have sexual intercourse via vaginal penetration with corpses. Is this accurate, John?"

"Yes, I do have a strong desire to fuck dead females."

"Why do you have such a strong desire for this?"

"I have been turned down so many times by females; I have to satisfy my intense feeling of getting 'laid'. Dead females don't complain; they don't turn me down, and I can fuck them. I can satisfy my feeling of the need to have my cock in a pussy with them. I no longer need to masturbate with my hand."

"Have you experienced vaginal intercourse with a corpse, John?"

"No, not yet! I am trying to get the orderly to let me in the morgue. It isn't going to hurt the corpse, so why won't he let me down there?"

"John, we are going to work with you to help in understanding a healthy sexual relationship vs. an unhealthy sexual relationship of which you have been subjected to and desire. There is a big difference, and you will discover a healthy sexual relationship, with live females, is paramount and so much more fulfilling than what you have encountered. Are you willing, John, to work with us and make changes?"

"Sure, I will try."

DICKERSON'S MORTUARY SERVICES

A couple of years pass and John Dickerson has been released from the Moravia State Institution Of The Mentally Insane with a supposed clean bill of mental health.

"John, congratulations on your new endeavor as a Mortuary Service and taking over my business," says Mr. Liberty.

"My pleasure and thank you, Mr. Liberty. I hope you aren't too upset about me changing the name of the business."

"John, it is your business now. I would think you would want to change the name of the business to make it your own," says Mr. Liberty.

"Mr. Liberty, I will have the down payment for this building by the first of the next month," says John.

"John, don't be so presumptuous. It takes time to build a business. Clients may know to come to this building, but the change in the name of the services and the mortician will take time to win them over to do business with you."

"Mr. Liberty, I plan to price my services so that they will be compelled to use my services."

"Remember, John; it is not just the pricing. It has a lot more to do with how you treat your clients and give them what they need in their time of bereavement. You have to be very careful with your client's loved ones who will be lying on your table. Treat the bodies with respect and make sure your work shows you cared enough to dress them out perfectly for the calling hours. You will find it very difficult with some of the bodies you get, but you always must make sure they look pleasing to the grieving family."

"I understand Mr. Liberty. I will be in touch with you next month," says John.

TREVOR'S VISIT

J ohn announces his new business to Trevor and discusses his slim chances of getting a female to have sexual relations.

"Hey, John, congratulations on your new business, and look at that sign, 'Dickerson's Mortuary Services'; very classy!" exclaims Trevor.

"Thanks, Trevor. Where do you stand with a new business of your own?" asks John.

"I am not starting a business, at least for now. I have teamed up with Frederick's Mortuary Services as a partner Mortician, although I sometimes wonder if I am a partner. I get all of the 'dirty' work. How are you doing with your female dating, John?" asks Trevor.

"Not so well. Harford is a small town, and there aren't many chicks, here. The ones that are here have turned me down."

"That's not so great. I hear the Harford Police Chief is a real looker. How about trying your luck with her?"

"Hell, no! Not her! I agree she is a real looker, but to be able to get into her panties...fat chance!" exclaims John.

"You never know until you try, John."

"Look, I already met her, and she is at least in her mid-thirties."

"What is the matter with that John? Her pussy doesn't have an age, at least yet. She has plenty of lubrication, I am sure," states Trevor.

"Trevor, she is too old for me. I want the ones in their twenties," says John.

"Good luck in finding them in this small town. As I said, maybe you should start dating the corpses you bring in," suggests Trevor.

"OK, OK, Trevor, I have work to do in getting things ready for my first client and the corpse. I will talk to you later."

NEW GUY IN TOWN

Conversations at the Police Department in Harford discuss the new Mortuary, Nicole's baby, and Bobbie's desire to have more children.

"Julia, did you see we have a new business in town; I mean a new Mortuary?" asks Bobbie.

"Yes, Bobbie, I met him yesterday. His name is John Dickerson. He seems to be a pleasant guy, but Morticians are creepy to me, and I feel there is something sinister about him. I must say during our brief conversation, he seemed to be eyeing me over pretty thoroughly," says Julia.

"As I have always said, Julia, you are beautiful, and guys know it too!"

"Don't get any ideas, Bobbie! I am quite happy living as a widow."

"By the way, how are Nicole and her baby daughter?" asks Bobbie.

"Nicole is doing just fine with her studies, and she is such a great mom for Becky. I must say that I enjoy having them around and,

Becky, well she is just a sweetheart. It won't be long before she is walking. How is little Julia, Bobbie?"

"She is growing like a weed, and she can almost stand up without help. I bet she will be walking soon, as well. Her personality is just like Richard's. I can see the deviltry in her eyes," says Bobbie.

"Time to have another one, Bobbie?" asks Julia.

"No, no, not yet! Richard and I have some catching up to do behind closed doors if you know what I mean."

"Careful, Bobbie, those little 'swimmers' might find their target, again…"

"I know, I know, Julia," says Bobbie.

THE FIRST CLIENT

T he calls start to come in to Dickerson's Mortuary for services, and John Dickerson gets his first client for his new business.

"Hello, Dickerson's Mortuary, how may I help you?" asks John.

"It's my daughter. She has been sick, and the doctors have told us she has only a limited time to live. We want to set up funeral arrangements, now, if that is possible," says Linda.

"Certainly, why don't you stop by at your convenience and we will discuss your needs," says John.

"Is tomorrow afternoon a good time?"

"Sure, why don't you come over at two in the afternoon. Don't worry, Linda, we will make sure your daughter is well taken care of when the need comes. I am to assume you do not want your daughter cremated and wish to have her laid out for open casket calling hours?" asks John.

"Yes, that is our wish."

John's First Client Arrives

"Mr. Dickerson, our daughter has been sick for a very long time. It is her lungs, Cystic Fibrosis, and she has taken a turn for the worse. We knew her time was coming, but we had wished not this soon," explains Linda.

"What is your daughter's name?" asks John.

"Her name is Lynn, and she is just twenty-two years old, the poor dear. Such a waste..such a waste," says Linda, trying not to cry.

"How do you want to proceed? I am assuming you want calling hours; an open casket?" asks John.

"Yes, we were thinking of a birch casket. We aren't very rich, and we don't have insurance," says Linda.

"She would look so much better in a cherry casket. Is she blonde, brunette, or redhead?"

"She is a brunette."

"Cherry would be the way to go," says John.

"Cherry would be nice, but the expense," says Linda.

"Let's see, a birch casket's price is fifteen hundred dollars, and cherry would be in the range of twenty-five hundred dollars," says John.

"Oh, we can't afford the cherry casket," says Linda.

"Look, do you have a burial plot for Lynn?"

"No, we don't."

"I normally charge around fifteen hundred dollars for a burial plot. Here is what I can do for you. If you would like the cherry casket for Lynn, I will throw in the burial plot for nothing extra," says John.

"We wanted to have her buried, here, in the Harford Cemetery, but we were told there is no room," says Linda.

"That is no problem. I can get Lynn into the Harford Cemetery."

"Oh, that would be so wonderful!" exclaims Linda.

"OK, so the casket is to be cherry, and you will supply me with the burial clothes?" asks John.

"Yes, and could you braid her hair? She loves to braid her hair, and we think she will be happy if you can do that for us, and her," says Linda.

"Yes, certainly."

"Are there more charges we will be responsible for, like your services for dressing, makeup, etc.?" asks Linda.

"I only charge five hundred dollars for those. I do not hire those services out. I will take care of picking Lynn up from your home when the need arises, and I will take her to the cemetery. I will handle everything for you. Lynn will be in good hands and well taken care of," says John.

"Thank you so much," says Linda.

DEATH HAS ARRIVED AT THE DOORSTEP

John thinks back on Trevor's suggestion of having sexual relations with a corpse and feels that it might not be so bad, after all. He once thought about it before the Institution.

"Dickerson's Mortuary?"

"Yes, this is John, how may I help you?"

"This is Linda, Linda Paisley. We spoke about my poor daughter, Lynn, a few weeks back."

"Yes, Mrs. Paisley, I remember."

"My Lynn has passed on to the heavenly gates, says Linda, crying."

"I will be over to pick Lynn up. You are at 112 Waverley, is that correct?" asks John.

"Yes."

"Please have ready the outfit you would like to have your daughter wear for the calling hours. I am assuming you want calling hours for your daughter?"

"Yes, we do. I will give you the outfit when you come to pick her up."

BACK AT THE MORTUARY

"Well, Lynn, you are quite beautiful!" John says to himself.

John hesitates as he thinks of the steps involved in preparing the body; being that Lynn is his first corpse since graduating from college. John decides he will record his preparations to enable him to recall proper procedures for the next body.

"OK, I need to make sure that the corpse is warm. I don't want to have Rigor Mortis set in too quickly. I have a lot of work ahead of me. First, I need to wash the body. It isn't too difficult due to her wearing a bathrobe. OK, off with the bra and panties. My God, I am so familiar with tits and ass, but never on a dead girl, although, they don't look any different to me."

John becomes so engrossed with his work; he forgets he is recording his every word.

"Trevor said, 'why don't I just ask a corpse out on a date'. I can see where that could be very beneficial to me and satisfy my cravings for sex. I don't have to ask her for a date because here she is, right in front of me and she has allowed me even to undress her. I wonder if I can actually, well, I don't know. Will it feel the same? Her tits are nice and warm, and one benefit is her nipples are erect, and she isn't even cold. I like that! Better to suck on! What about her pussy? It is warm too, but not too wet. Let's see, what do I have. Yes, this will do for now, but I can see I will need to order some gel lubricant for vaginas. OK, I insert this turkey baster into her vagina and squeeze some in there. Great, now to suck on her tits and massage her clit. I miss the moans, but I am getting hard. Next, to spread her legs and mount her. I am not used to the unresponsiveness, but I do like that I can do what I want without complaints. Oh, yeah, her pussy is well lubricated and still warm. If I were to close my eyes I could swear I am fucking a live girl! I wonder if a vagina gets Rigor Mortis? We didn't go over that in

29

the lab, but would we have? I better get to my business just in case Rigor Mortis does affect the vagina and I will not be able to pull out. Ah, here it comes. Blast away! Sweetheart, your pussy is so tight; I bet you were a virgin. Oh, shit, I need to finish bathing her, and oh, I need to let my load run out of her pussy. It can't be running out of her during calling hours. I have a lot to do; wash her hair; braid it; dress her; pose her in the typical casket arrangement, hands crossed just below her tits on her chest. Yup, eyes are closed. The last thing I must do is embalm her and put her in the casket. Some light eye makeup; a little rouge on her cheeks and some lipstick after I give her a passionate kiss. I am so glad Trevor brought the subject up of dating my corpses. I can see where it can satisfy my hunger for sex between live females."

LAURIE LIBBY

John has gotten used to having sex with his female corpses but misses the interaction only a live female can give. One day, while over in Cloverville, he meets Laurie Libby. He decides he won't come on so strong in the beginning, because he desperately needs the live interaction. Besides, with the pricing he has been giving out for his services, he has picked up many clients from all over the adjoining towns to Harford. He is sure he will have another young female corpse to sink his dick into rather soon.

"Oh, let me pick that up for you," says John.

"Thank you, I am so clumsy. I have all of these papers to file. I shouldn't have taken so many at one time," says Laurie.

"Think nothing of it. By the way, my name is John Dickerson. What may I ask is yours?"

"I am Laurie, Laurie Libby. I have just moved here, in Cloverville, a couple of weeks ago."

"Very nice to meet you. My home is in Harford."

"What brings you to Cloverville?" asks Laurie.

"Oh, just visiting an old college friend of mine."

"What college did you and your friend attend?"

"We went to Claire Bethany School of Mortuary Sciences."

"Oh, my, so you are a Mortician?"

"Yes, I am the Mortician over at Dickerson's Mortuary Services in Harford. I hope that doesn't scare you."

"Ah, no, but being a Mortician is different."

"Someone has to bury the dead, don't they, respectfully?" asks John.

"Yes, I suppose they do."

"What is your occupation, Miss Libby?"

"Oh, you can call me Laurie. I am a court stenographer."

"That sure sounds interesting. Do you have a ......?"

"Husband? No, I am not married. Not many men are interested in court stenographers. How about you?"

"No, not many women are interested in marrying a Mortician. They probably think it is creepy."

JOHN NOTICES WHILE IN CONVERSATION, LAURIE'S FEMALE PROPORTIONS ARE JUST RIGHT. AMPLE TITS AND AN ASS WHICH NEEDS FUCKING. HE SO WANTS TO FUCK HER, BUT HE HAS TO WORK ON HIS PLAN TO HAVE HER STAY AROUND FOR HIM. HE WILL GET HIS CHANCE, SOON. HE HOPES HE WILL GET A CORPSE SOON SO THAT HE CAN RELEASE HIS DESIRES

"Miss Libby, I mean Laurie, would it be right of me if I were to ask you to dinner tonight?"

"Quite possible, but dinner would need to be quite early, because I have an early court case tomorrow morning."

"Strange you should say that because I have work to do tomorrow morning as well," says John.

"Another body?" asks Laurie.

"No, so how about seven tonight? Is that early enough?"

"Oh, yes," says Laurie.

"Great, I will meet you at the Great Bull restaurant on Harrison," says John.

JOHN MAKES HIS MOVE AT DINNER

J ohn finds a great prospect in a living female.

"John, thank you so much for the wonderful dinner and conversation. I feel I have gotten to know you better and you don't appear to me as being creepy!"

"Thanks, Laurie. I have enjoyed learning more about you as well."

"We should be going. I have to get up early tomorrow morning," says Laurie.

"Laurie, may I walk you home?"

"I live in an apartment just around the corner. I can manage."

"Please, I insist," says John.

"John, how often do you travel here to Cloverville?"

"Quite a few times; I have clients here as well."

"Next time you are here, maybe we will run into each other," says Laurie.

"Could I ask you if you would be willing to come to dinner with me on Friday evening?" asks John.

"That would be terrific! Seven, again?"

"Yes, ma'am," says John.

GETTING OFF

After saying goodnight to Laurie, John walks speedily back to his car to travel back to Harford.

Once underway, he cannot stop visualizing Laurie, naked, on his bed with his torso nestled between her legs. He reaches down to his groin and feels his hardness expanding. He stops on the side of the road and opens his car door.

"Oh, ah, oh…. Yes…yes……!"

Panting rapidly, he shuts his car door and continues to Harford, muttering to himself, "I can't do that! I need a woman for this, not my hand. Laurie, you need to be the woman for me!"

GETTING SERIOUS

J ohn has dinner once a week with Laurie, and in between her work and his, phone conversations are regular.

AFTER DINNER ONE NIGHT

"John, please, oh please!" exclaims Laurie as if to beg.

"I assume a kiss is what you were begging?"

"Yes, John, I have wanted to kiss you almost since I first laid eyes on you."

"Laurie, you don't know how many times I wanted to kiss you. I was hoping for the opportunity."

"John, dear, you didn't have to wait for an opportunity. It just prolonged my agony."

"Come here, Laurie! Agonize no further!"

"John, all of this kissing can lead to more, you know. I want you to know I am a proper lady and if you have any intentions of going further with me, well, you will need to marry me first."

"Laurie, are you proposing marriage to me?"

"I just wanted you to know I am a proper lady."

"Well, then, Laurie, will you marry me and be my wife?"

"More agony! I thought you would never ask. Oh, yes, I will be your wife!"

Marriage was not part of John's plan. He did not want to be tied down. He was a 'one-night stand' type of guy, but what the hell, Laurie would always be available to fuck any time he wanted. He did think he could get bored fucking her, but then again, he had his corpses...quite a variety of pussies.

CHANGE OF PLANS

J ohn's sexual desires drive him to beg Laurie to move their wedding day sooner.

"John, there is no way we can move the wedding up to next month. We talked about the schedule, and we both agreed it would be best for the wedding to be four months from now," says Laurie.

"But, honey, I am having a lot of trouble, ya know. You being a proper lady and all, kind of puts a huge strain on my sexual prowess," says John.

"What did you do about your sexual prowess before you met me? I suggest you take matters in hand and wait for the real thing," says Laurie.

"Can we move it up a month and a half?" asks John.

"No, John. Don't you have some corpses to attend to?"

"No, I don't, Laurie. I thought you would be open to some compromise!"

"John, I tell you what, if you can live without seeing me for a week or two so I can concentrate on the wedding arrangements, I believe we could get married in two months instead of four. Can you do that for me, John?"

"Yes, I promise! Thank you, my sweet dear," says John.

BACK IN THE SADDLE

J ohn meets the Coroner, Sam, and gets more prospects to satisfy
his sexual desires.

"Mr. John Dickerson?"

"Yes, this is John."

"My name is Sam, and I am the coroner for Harford and
surrounding counties. We haven't met yet, but I have three bodies I
need to transport to your mortuary. All three females were involved
in a car accident, and I do not need autopsies. When can I bring
them by?"

"Sam, how about three this afternoon?"

"Sounds good. I will see you then."

SAM TRAVELS TO DICKINSON'S MORTUARY

"Hello, John?"

"Yes, Sam, please come in. It is nice to meet you."

"I am glad that you have picked up the business from Mr. Liberty. He was getting picky in his old age and would only accept some of my bodies. I had to travel all the way over to Jackson City to a Mortuary over there."

"Sam, I am glad to be able to assist you, and I will be more than glad to take all of the bodies you have in the future. My goal is to be the Mortuary of choice for Harford and the surrounding counties. I keep my prices better than competitive, and I take the extra time to cater to the families of their lost loved ones."

"What happened to these poor girls; they are so young," says John.

"All three were riding in a limousine on the way to a senior ball, I believe, when a dump truck ran a red light and 'T' boned them. They never had a chance. Seventeen and eighteen-years of age, it appears," says Sam.

"It will take some work on their faces," says John.

"Yeah unfortunately, all three died of broken necks."

"Sam, what about family? Have they been notified?"

"The Chief of Police, Miss Julia Lillus, currently is trying to contact their parents. It appears all of their parents are abroad," says Sam.

"I will need to put them in a storage locker until their parents can be notified and I get instructions from them on how they wish me to proceed. It can't be for more than two days, or I will need to dress them out before I won't be able to," says John.

"Here, Sam, let me help you with them. I have three tables, here, to lay them on. Let me know as soon as you hear about the whereabouts of their parents," says John.

"OK, John, I will. You might hear from the Chief before I hear. Nice meeting you and I will see you again, soon," says Sam.

AS SOON AS SAM LEAVES THE MORTUARY, JOHN QUICKLY GOES OVER TO WHERE THE THREE GIRLS LAY

———

"Hmm, nice! I have a blonde, redhead, and a brunette. Let's see what is hiding under those dresses. Nice panties, I must say! Those lace bikini panties sure turn be on, and oh, one has black, and the other two have red. I get a hard-on just looking at them. Let me peak under here. Shaved pussies; all three," mutters John to himself.

John fills the turkey baster with vaginal lubricating gel and inserts it into the vagina of the redheaded female corpse.

"Let's see, the redhead tonight, the brunette in the morning, and I will save the blonde for tomorrow afternoon's dessert!" exclaims John.

———

THE EVENING ARRIVES AND JOHN STARES AT THE REDHEADED GIRL ON THE TABLE

———

He touches his penis as he unhooks her bra and cups his hands around her breasts. He is amazed by her nipples standing erect after he sucks on them. As soon as his penis is stiffened, John climbs on the table and spreads her legs as he mounts her and thrusts himself into her 'glory hole'.

"Damn, she has a tight pussy! Only one, two…. ah….ah…," his load exits his penis and lines her love tunnel.

"Man, she 'grasped my shaft' so well, I only had to thrust three times before I exploded into her. Good job, sweetheart!" as he bends down and kisses her lips.

———

John is very pleased the fuck with the brunette, and the blonde gave similar results for him. He hopes he can get more female corpses within the next four weeks to satisfy his sexual desires; then it is 'onto' Laurie.

A STRANGE TURN OF EVENTS

It has been a full week, and John has not taken in any new female corpses. He thinks about the three girls he fucked and wished they could still be around to continue satisfying his sexual addiction. The trouble with dead bodies is they don't stay around for very long.

One morning when John purchases a newspaper, he reads that an inmate in the Jackson City Prison is due for parole on Friday of the week.

FRIDAY MORNING ARRIVES, AND JOHN IS IN HIS CAR OUTSIDE THE JACKSON CITY PRISON GATES, WAITING

"Hey you over there! Need a ride?" asks John.

"Who the hell are you and what do you want?"

"I am offering you a ride to wherever you need to go," says John.

"OK, so why are you giving me a ride?"

"Well, first things first. Now please get in the car," says John.

"Who are you?"

"My name is John Dickerson of Dickerson's Mortuary in Harford."

"Oh, great, I am riding with an undertaker!"

"And what is your name?" asks John.

"My name is Joe Lindsey. They call me 'Joe the Ripper'."

"Why is that, Joe?"

"It is the reason I have been in this hell hole. I have murdered quite a few women in my time, after raping them," says Joe.

"So, you are a reformed man now?" asks John.

"Well, let's put it this way. I am out on good behavior. They believed me when I told them I had 'learned my lesson' while doing my time here."

"Joe, the main reason I am giving you a ride is that I have a proposition for you," says John.

"Yup, there is always a reason for sudden hospitality. So, what is it you want?" asks Joe.

"Let's say I am a new business in Harford and I need clients to stay in business. I want to be the biggest and best Mortuary Service in Harford and all surrounding counties including Jackson City. For that to happen, I need bodies; dead bodies."

"Yeah, where do I come in for that?" asks Joe.

"I am hoping that you might take up my offer to partner with me to supply me with the corpses."

"How do you figure I can supply them for you? What do I get out of this?"

"Joe, you have a 'knack' for finding dead bodies, don't you?" asks John.

"Well, yeah. The ones I killed."

"I am not interested in the how, but only the inflow of corpses into my Mortuary. I don't want to know or care how it is accomplished, but...," says John.

"Look, if you are suggesting I kill bodies for you, to build your business, I don't think I am interested," says Joe.

"Maybe you should think more of a human process, like natural causes of death. You could genuinely date some females and, well, they might get hooked and overdose," suggests John.

"If that be the case, all you would get from me is females. I am not into men dating."

"No matter, all I need is corpses."

"You haven't mentioned what is in it for me, and it will be a steep price if I go along with your proposition," says Joe.

"OK Joe, you can fuck any of them you want, and I will give you two hundred dollars a corpse you bring me," says John.

"I am sorry, but four hundred a head is my price," responds Joe.

"I will pay two hundred a head for the ordinary; four hundred a head for the twenty-year-old females; and one hundred a head for the thirty-year-old females. No corpses older and all corpses must be clean and not beaten, cut or otherwise. I can only make money by doing very little prep work for showing at calling hours," says John.

"Say I agree to your terms; how will I not be suspect of foul play?" asks Joe.

"You will hide behind the deaths 'due to natural causes'; and you will have to wear a condom every time you fuck one of them. There can be no DNA trace if rape is suspected. All you need to do is cause the natural death; and the coroner and I will do the rest," says John.

"Sounds reasonable to me. I get to continue to get 'laid' and make money at the same time. Are you sure you can afford four hundred dollars a head?"

"Just bring me the corpses, and you will get paid," says John.

"When do you want me to start?" asks Joe.

"Tonight! I will drop you off at the local strip club to get you started," says John.

PLENTY OF PUSSY

S am is bringing in a lot of young female corpses to the Mortuary and John contemplates how to handle the situation once married to Laurie.

"Sam, what is it?" asks John.

"John, I have a female down here at the strip club. She overdosed on an opiate, it appears. These young people! I don't get it."

"OK Sam, bring her here and try to find her parents or someone who cares for her," says John.

"I am afraid these girls are going to be what we call 'loners'. We never seem to be able to locate the next of kin or parents. It is like they divorce themselves from those strip club girls," says Sam.

John has had two corpses from the local strip club, and then he starts getting corpses from across town. He is happy Joe is mixing it up where they come from to not show a pattern.

The girls range from twenty years of age to twenty-eight years of age and are very clean with no signs of recent vaginal penetration.

John wonders what he will do with this scheme once married to Laurie. He could disband it or keep it going along with fucking Laurie. After all, he has grown quite fond of fucking corpses.

SOMETHING DOESN'T ADD UP

Back at the office, Bobbie, Richard, and Julia start to see a pattern in young female deaths due to drug overdoses.

"Bobbie and Richard take a look at these drug overdose cases that have seemed to increase lately," says Chief Julia Lillus.

"I am not sure if I detect a pattern, but it does seem strange. Maybe there is a drug ring infiltrating the city and surrounding counties," says Bobbie.

"Two of the girls are from the strip club, here, in Harford," says Julia.

"Take a look at their ages. All of them are between twenty and twenty-nine years of age," says Richard.

"Well, one thing for sure is our new Mortuary Services is having a boon in business," says Bobbie.

"We will keep an eye on this and see if a pattern develops. Meanwhile, Richard, I need you to scout around the strip clubs in the area and see if you can detect a drug ring developing. Bobbie, I want you to nose around and see if there is some peculiar activity with twenty-year-old females in the area, such as significant dates, etc. Hey, by the way, did you guys get the 'updated' wedding invitation to John Dickerson's and Laurie Libby's wedding? They were getting married four months from now in the first invitation, and now they are getting married next month," says Julia.

"Yeah, we did. I guess there are others who are so hot they need to get married right away!" exclaims Bobbie.

"Oh, you mean like you and Richard? My understanding is you were almost climaxing, Bobbie, as you were walking down the aisle, and you, Richard; let's say it was pretty evident where your mind was," says Julia.

"No way, Julia! Nothing was showing! Bobbie were you climaxing walking down the aisle?" asks Richard.

"It is possible! I know I had to change my panties immediately following our vows. It was very uncomfortable with wet panties, and no I did not pee my panties," explains Bobbie.

THE MARRIAGE OF JOHN DICKERSON

J ohn and Laurie are married and John cannot wait to get Laurie in bed.

"Finally, Laurie, our day has arrived," says John.

"You see, John, it wasn't so hard to wait the two months, was it?" asks Laurie.

"I guess not."

"Do you, John Dickerson, take Laurie Libby to be your lawfully wedded...."

"Do you, Laurie Libby, take John Dickerson to be your lawfully wedded...."

"I would like to announce you, man and wife. You may kiss the bride."

AFTER THE CEREMONY AND BEFORE THE RECEPTION

"Mrs. Dickerson, I have waited for this moment forever. Come over here and lie down."

"Mr. Dickerson, we are going to be needed out on the floor of the reception for our first dance. We do not have too much time."

"Honey, It will be OK! Now lie down here. Yes, position yourself just like that."

"John, what are you going to do to me in such a short time?"

"Just wait and see!"

"Oh, John, you sure know how to turn on a girl. Oh…...ohhhh!" Laurie moans as John suckles her nipples while caressing her clit with his fingers.

Laurie's wetness intensifies as John's cock stiffens. John removes his fingers from Laurie's pussy and penetrates her with care.

"Oh….ohhh..ooohh," moans Laurie.

"John, I guess you do know how to screw. Are you sure you haven't had any practice?"

"I swear to God, I haven't. It is because of you sweetheart! You turn me on!"

John continues while Laurie starts to move her hips in concert with his motion. She reaches down to her 'clit' and begins to massage it with her finger as John is thrusting his penis into her vagina.

"Here we go, Mrs. Dickerson! I am about to make my mark!" John states just as his load empties into her. Shortly after, Laurie 'cums' after massaging her clit.

They both lay, there, on the bed briefly, to enjoy the intensity of their climaxes.

"Well, Mrs. Dickerson, I have made my mark. You are officially mine, now."

"Yes, Mr. Dickerson, I knew waiting for this moment would be well worth it!"

"Well, get used to it, because as soon as we are free, later, tonight, we will be revisiting ourselves much more closely when we have more time," says John.

"OK, John, but for now, I need to let your semen leak out from my vagina, so it isn't running down my leg on our first dance."

"Hey, nobody will be able to see it with the long gown. It might be quite sexy, ya know," says John.

"Sure, Ok, I will make sure on our next encounter to allow it to leak out onto your leg and then you can walk around and see how it feels," says Laurie.

THE HARFORD POLICE DEPARTMENT

A pattern appears to show up with the events in the Community of Harford.

"Julia, I think I am starting to see a pattern, here, with the deaths due to drug overdoses," says Bobbie.

"How is that, Bobbie?" asks Julia.

"The deaths are mounting, as you know. All of the overdoses are females in their twenties, and the deaths appear to be in all counties revolving around Harford. I feel there is a reason all deaths are young females and only in a finite area. Did you hear from Sam what drugs are causing the overdose?" asks Bobbie.

"Yes, Sam has told me that all overdoses, so far, are opiates. He also feels that some, if not all of the females, have been raped or at least had consensual penetration," says Julia.

"What about DNA results?" asks Bobbie.

"Sam says there are no signs of DNA differences other than the victim's; specifically tests from their vagina's. He feels if those girls have been penetrated in some fashion; condoms were used and the penetrator was very neat. There were no signs of semen. He did find signs of blood and some had indications their hymens were broke at the time of their deaths," says Julia.

"All of those female corpses have been brought to Dickerson's, at least so far. I don't feel anything is going on there, at this point, and many of the girls who I have interviewed, reported to me a man they had not seen before was taking girls out on dates. We need to be able to connect those women with the corpses if any," says Bobbie.

"Bobbie, we need to do some more role-playing. Do you think you are up to it?" asks Julia.

"I am not sure, Julia, it depends upon what you have in mind."

"Oh, no, here we go again, she almost got raped, again, with the last role-play," says Richard.

"The role-playing I have in mind won't be quite as dangerous. Bobbie, do you still have ties with those four cadets in your officer training classes?" asks Julia.

"Yes, I talk to them now and then."

"Here is what I have in mind, Bobbie. I need you to frequent the strip club down the street and blend in as a customer who..."

"Likes to watch, Julia?" asks Bobbie.

"Bobbie, you won't be alone because I, too, will be a customer who likes to watch, but we won't be at the club at the same time or day," says Julia.

"It sounds like we are going on a 'fishing trip'!" exclaims Bobbie.

"Yes, Bobbie, we need to set the 'hooks' and see if we can catch our 'fish'."

"What part of your plan involves the cadets?" asks Bobbie.

"I want each cadet to frequent a different strip club or bar in the surrounding counties. They, too, will 'like to watch'," says Julia.

"The only problem I see so far Julia, if we are trying to catch this guy, he seems to only date girls in their twenties. In case you haven't noticed, I am almost beyond that age group and a mother," says Bobbie.

"I have the same problem, but I think if we dress appropriately with the right makeup, he can't resist to ask us on a date. We are quite young looking even though you are reaching into your late twenties and me in my late thirties," says Julia.

"Yeah, I agree with Julia! You ladies are 'hot'!" exclaims Richard.

"Richard!" exclaims Bobbie.

"If and when we are approached with a proposition to date, our conversation will try to steer the acceptance of a date to a party. We will need to make it clear we want the party to include hallucinogenic drugs," says Julia.

"What if we are asked to date by different individuals?" asks Bobbie.

"It is always a possibility, but I have a feeling the dating propositions will be from the same guy," answers Julia.

"OK, so we happen to get asked on a date by the same guy, what are we going to do then?" asks Bobbie.

"I am sure he won't want to have a party date with all of us at once. The track record we see appears to be 'one-on-one' dates. My hunch is, during the dates, this guy will introduce an opiate to bring our inhibitions down and then proceed to rape each of us. At the finish of the rape, he will inject enough opiate to cause death," says Julia.

"Julia, how can you be so sure the chain of events during the dates?" asks Richard.

"Well, it is just a hunch, but in talking to Sam, his initial observations showed no bruising, a sign of there being no struggle, and one needle mark located in the same general area on the thigh of each victim. He noted particles of opiate in each of the victim's stomach which led him to believe the initial drug dosage was ingested, probably from a drink," says Julia.

"How are we to play the role and not ingest any drugs or actually be raped?" asks Bobbie.

"We will have to lead him to believe we are already high on opiates. He will know he cannot give us more opiates because it would cause death. We will not cooperate with him, which will foil his plan to proceed in his desire to rape. It appears he cannot cause a struggle, so I believe he will end the date," says Julia.

"What happens if none of what you say happens and it turns dangerous to us?" asks Bobbie.

"Each of us will wear a 'bug' and Richard will be outside in view of the dating place in case there are altercations. He will step in and have the guy arrested for attempted assault, therefore we must be sure to force schedule the date on different days," says Julia.

"Julia, as you were relaying the supposed actions taken during the date, I thought of something that was right in front of my face!"

"What is it, Richard?"

"You are saying Sam has looked at each of the victim's bodies and noticed no signs of struggle and almost no sign of rape. Why is that? Who gets the victim's bodies after the Coroner, Sam, is finished with his observations? Of course, the Mortician!" Richard exclaims.

"Now, why does the Mortician need a 'clean' and unaltered corpse, be it all females?" asks Julia.

"You have a point, Richard," says Bobbie.

"I believe I will take a ride over to Dickerson's Mortuary tomorrow morning and see what I can find out. Meanwhile, Bobbie, get in touch with your cadet friends and go shopping for some provocative clothing," says Julia.

"Bobbie, whatever you do, don't ruin the provocative clothing you buy for this role-play charade. You can use it with me and I promise I won't feed you any opiates to get my way!" exclaims Richard.

"Richard, I am warning you! You had better have your mind on listening in on us during our dates! Julia what am I going to do with him?"

"Bobbie, just cherish the feelings he has for you! He is such a great lover for you; take it all in and keep it close to your heart," says Julia.

DICKERSON'S MORTUARY IS DISTURBING

L aurie is not happy living above the Mortuary and expresses it to John.

"John, do you really feel we have to live, here, in this Mortuary? Maybe we should find a house or apartment close by for our residence," says Laurie.

"Why, Laurie? It is so convenient for us to be living here. I can perform my work more competitively here," says John.

"This place gives me the creeps knowing that just under our bedroom there are dead people, corpses. I can even smell the stench of formaldehyde up here in our bedroom. Every time we get into sexual activity, I can't help to think those corpses are listening to us!" exclaims Laurie.

"Sweetheart, they are dead! They can't hear us!"

"Why, John, are you taking in so many corpses lately? The sheer number of them being here, creeps me out even more."

"Honey, those corpses are our bread and butter. I want to be the number one Mortician in the area. We can certainly use the money, especially due to the fact that I have just started Mortuary Services right out of college. Most do not have the opportunity that I have."

"I know, John, and I am proud of you, but do you think we could try to find a residence away from this building?"

"We can think about it more after my business takes route," says John.

JULIA MAKES A VISIT

J ulia pulls up in front of Dickerson's Mortuary and rings the parlor doorbell.

"Hello, my name is Julia Lillus. I am the Police Chief for the Harford Police Department," says Julia

"Oh, hello, I am Laurie, Mr. Dickerson's wife."

"Yes, congratulations! I am sorry I was unable to attend your wedding, but police work never seems to end. I am here to speak to your husband, John."

"Oh, yes, please come in," says Laurie.

"John, my dear, the Police Chief is here to speak to you."

"OK, Laurie, please send her into the parlor," says John.

"Nice to see you, Chief Lillus. What brings you here?" asks John.

"I wanted to stop by to congratulate you and your new wife on your recent wedding and relate to you how happy I am for your growing business here in Harford. We are a small community and a booming business such as yours, is really healthy for our community," says Julia.

"Thank you. I want to be able to be the Mortuary Services for all, due to my competitive prices, but more so, catering to the needs of the bereaved," says John.

"I hear you are doing fairly well. As you know, we have had a rash of overdoses lately, which brings to you quite a bit of business. I am sorry the Department is having trouble in locating the families of the victims. Quite a few of the victims have no ties to relatives that we can find," says Julia.

"It is too bad. I don't have much of a window in dressing out the corpses for the next of kin to be found. Most are closed casket anyway with no calling hours," says John.

SUDDENLY, THERE IS A KNOCK AT THE DOOR OF THE MORTUARY

"John, I hate to interrupt, but I have a guy here by the name of Joe, who wants to talk to you about the corpses," says Laurie interrupting.

"Thank you, dear, I will be out in a minute. Just tell him to wait in the entryway," says John.

JOHN EXCUSES HIMSELF FROM JULIA AND GOES TO TALK WITH JOE. WHEN JOHN OPENS THE DOOR FROM THE PARLOR, JULIA IS ABLE TO SEE TO THE ENTRYWAY AND NOTICES JOE STANDING THERE.

"Joe, what the hell are you doing coming here during the day?" asks John angrily.

"I..I.."

"Shush, not so loud. The Police Chief is in the parlor visiting," says John.

"Why is she here?" asks Joe.

"It is none of your business, Joe. Now what do you want?"

"I have seen some pretty 'hot' chicks in the bars and strip clubs around here. They look as if they might be pushing thirty years of age, but they are 'hot' and could easily be taken to be in their twenties. I want to know if they can be of use to you?"

"Joe, use your judgment. As long as they do not need much work, go ahead, but do not make it a habit to bring those corpses to me."

"I will have fun fucking them," says Joe.

"Remember what I told you, Joe. Now get out of here and don't ever come here during the day, again!"

"I apologize, Chief Lillus. He is a pesky guy bugging me about employment. He tells me he can embalm, but I do my own embalming. Anyhow, where were we?" asks John.

"I was just congratulating you on your new booming business and apologize for my lack of speediness in getting contact information to you for the influx of corpses you have," says Julia.

"No need to apologize, Chief."

"Well, thank you for your time and be sure to let us know if we can be of any help to you and your business," says Julia.

"We will," says John.

PLANS SOLIDIFY IN THE DEPARTMENT

J ulia returns to the office with some very important information about the increase of corpses at Dickerson's Mortuary.

"Bobbie, Richard, please come into my office!" exclaims Julia.

"I just returned from visiting John Dickerson at the Mortuary. During the visit, John was interrupted by a guy supposedly looking for employment in embalming. I don't think John meant to leave the parlor door open, but I recognized the guy. He goes by the name of 'Joe the Ripper' whose real name is Joseph Lindsey. He was just released from the Jackson City Prison a couple of weeks ago. He was serving time for murder and rape," says Julia.

"Holy hell," says Richard. "This could shed a different light on our thoughts of the overdoses."

"Why would he be visiting Dickerson? I will bet it wasn't for a job," says Bobbie.

"As a matter of fact, I actually overheard their conversation. John was scolding him about showing up at the door in the daytime. Joe also was remarking something about some 'hot' chicks at the local bars and strip clubs. Bobbie, have you or your cadet friends been frequenting those establishments?" asks Julia.

"Two cadets have been, but not me," says Bobbie.

"I think we will lay back and let the cadets continue while we observe. Richard, you will need to be ready when they contact you on what time and days of their dates. As soon as you hear from them, I will schedule a visit to the establishment and observe. Bobbie, you can take the other date and establishment. I will give you a picture of 'Joe the Ripper' so you know who you are observing. We are not acting, but just observing. Bobbie, did you go over the role-playing plan with the cadets?" asks Julia.

"Yes, they understand completely," says Bobbie.

"I still do not understand how we will be able to tie these overdoses to this 'Joe the Ripper'?" asks Richard.

"We just have to see how it unravels. One step at a time, Richard," says Julia.

THE DATE

S usan has a date at the strip club while Richard and Julia keep in
touch with the events.

"Richard, I am at the strip club. You copy?" asks Julia.

"Copy, Julia."

"Richard, this is Susan. Do you copy?"

"Yes, loud and clear. Be sure to vocalize as much as you can so I
can intercept if I need too. Julia, cadet Susan is ready," says Richard.

Susan is about thirty years of age and wearing a low-cut blouse
with a mini-skirt and black fishnet stockings. Julia cannot believe
how young she looks.

"Richard, our guy has just showed up," says Julia over her
microphone hidden in her bra.

"Hey, sweetheart, can I buy you a drink?" asks Joe.

"Ya, who the hell are you? Got any opiates on you?" asks Susan.

"I might. You on any?"

"I just shot up, but I may need more."

"Look, honey, we can talk about it over there at that table."

"You know, you are quite beautiful! I would love to get to know you more."

"Oh, ya, how are you going to do that?"

"I am the dating type of guy and was hoping to ask you out."

"I am here now, so this must be a date, huh?"

"Man, you are high!"

"I am noticing those hot legs of yours. What ya got between them?"

"Wouldn't you like to know. Careful my 'beaver' bites!"

"What do you say we go to a place more comfortable and get to know each other more intimately?"

"Look, mister, you aren't going to get anywhere with me. I don't just fuck anyone, ya, know?"

"Are you always this way when you get high?"

"What way is that lover-boy?"

"Opiates are supposed to lower your inhibitions. You are acting hard to get! Are you sure you shot up?"

"Look, lover-boy, if I tell you I shot up, it means I shot up. Look, here, this needle did the trick."

"You shot that much stuff?"

"Yup, now what do you want to do? I bet I can pole dance better than those girls up there."

"Come with me!"

"Where we are going, lover-boy?"

"Just come on!"

"Richard, he appears to be taking Susan to a private viewing room. I will lose sight of them, so you need to be on your game!" exclaims Julia.

"I am on it, Julia."

"By the way, what is your name, honey?"

"My name is Susan. What is yours lover-boy?"

"Doesn't matter!"

"What are we doing in this room?"

"I am going to fuck you!"

"Hell, no! I will scream!"

"See this? You are going to get it if you scream."

"Julia, he is threatening her with something. It appears he is not baking off."

"Keep on it, Richard. I will go in there if I have to," says Julia.

"Now, listen to me and cooperate."

"I told you my 'beaver' bites!"

"Ouch, what was that?" asks Susan.

"Just a little present. I am not going to fuck you after all, bitch. You are not worth it!"

"Phew, Julia. He has backed off and is not going to rape her," says Richard.

"Thank God, Richard. I am going to follow him to see where he goes. He might be going to the bar down the street to meet our other cadet."

"Should I help Susan?" asks Richard.

"She will be fine. She will report to the office in a few hours. She has her car. Get over to the bar. I have a feeling he will be headed there," says Julia.

A DIFFERENT ARRANGEMENT

John Dickerson puts on his coat and hat heading to the strip club. Once there, he walks up to the bar.

"Hello, I am Doctor Fingerly. I was called by a guy who said his girl passed out here. He said something about her being high. She has a low-cut blouse and a mini-skirt with black fishnet stockings. Have you seen her?" asks John.

"Oh yeah, that chick. Man, she is a 'hot' one. He took her in the empty viewing room over there," says the bartender.

"I will go get her. She needs to dry out," says John.

John walks over to the empty private viewing room and sees a female slumped on the floor. He picks her up and places her over his shoulder while holding her legs just under her ass. John mutters, "God, this girl is the most beautiful I have ever seen for a corpse. I will surely fuck her tonight after Laurie goes to sleep."

"Hey, you got her OK, Doc? Man look at her ass!" exclaims the bartender.

John loads Susan in the car and drives back to the Mortuary. He carefully and quietly enters the back door to the examining room. He gently places her on the table.

LAURIE HEARS JOHN ENTER THE MORTUARY AND YELLS DOWN TO HIM FROM THE SECOND FLOOR BEDROOM

"John, did you go out?" asks Laurie.

"Yes, honey, I had to get some more rubbing alcohol. I am running out and this will do until the shipment comes in," says John.

"How long before you are done, John? I want to go to bed. I am really tired," says Laurie.

"I will be right up, soon, sweetheart," says John.

CAUGHT IN THE ACT

John quickly rushes over to Susan and swiftly starts to undress her. This is the first corpse still warm and he relishes in being able to fuck her just as if she were alive. He decides that he will not need as much vaginal lubricant for this one, so he loads minimal into the turkey baster. As he removes Susan's blouse and then her bra, he touches her nipples with his hands and gives them a little pinch between his fingers. Immediately they become erect. John cannot resists placing his lips on them and sucking. After satisfying himself with her nipples, he moves down to her skirt. After removing Susan's skirt and fishnet stockings, he anticipates what lies beneath her white lace panties. John gently grabs the waistline to her panties and slowly lowers them over her pubic area exposing rich black hair giving way to her clit and then down past the lips to her vagina. After removing her panties, he stares at her pussy as he gently places his fingers in reaching for its end.

John carefully hops up onto the table and spreads Susan's legs to unfold the lips of her vagina exposing the opening, so he can lower himself to her. He starts to rub his cock to get the stiffness required for penetration.

Suddenly, Laurie hears a knock at the entryway door to the parlor.

She quickly puts her bathrobe over her bare shoulders and fixes the ties to hide her nakedness.

"Hello, who is it?" asks Laurie.

"It is Joe. I was here the other day to talk to your husband."

"Oh, yes, but it is late. Can it wait until tomorrow morning?"

"No, unfortunately ma'am, it cannot wait."

"OK, please come in. John is down in the examining room. I will take you to him."

Laurie escorts Joe down the hall past the parlor and to the stairs to the examining room. Joe cannot help to notice Laurie's shapely figure showing through her bathrobe. He mutters, "You my lady are fuckable, very fuckable!"

Laurie and Joe arrive at the examining room door at the bottom of the stairs. Laurie knocks and announces Joe is there to see him. She turns the door handle and opens the door.

Immediately she sees John on top of a corpse, who is lying on a table, with his stiffened penis straight out of his pants and about to enter the corpse's vagina.

"John Dickerson! What in the world are you doing with that dead body? You are actually going to fuck that corpse? Oh my God...," says Laurie in disbelief.

Laurie falls to the floor unconscious.

"What the hell, John! This is why you wanted all of those girls? You are a real sick bastard!" exclaims Joe.

"All right everyone, stay where you are!" orders Julia as she blasts through the doorway.

"John Dickerson! Get down off that corpse, and for heaven's sake, put your dick back in your pants. No one, here, wants to see that! John Dickerson, you are under arrest for murder and rape! You have the right to remain silent and anything you say can and will be used against you in the court of law!" exclaims Julia.

"I haven't murdered anyone! Him, Joe over there, murdered the corpses!" exclaims John.

"You, John, masterminded this!" exclaims Joe.

"Joseph Lindsey, you are under arrest for murder! You have the right to remain silent and anything you say can and will be used against you in the court of law!" exclaims Julia.

Julia places handcuffs on the two and walks over to Susan lying on the table while Sam is covering her up and taking vital signs.

"Sam, her name is Susan and, oh my God, how is she?"

"Julia, she has the same needle stick on her thigh as the other corpses. I don't know how much drug has been injected and what kind. She is breathing with a very slow pulse," says Sam.

"Joe Lindsey, what drug did you inject into this woman?" asks Julia.

"I don't know, maybe an opiate of some sort. John gave me the drugs," answers Joe.

"John, what is the drug? You best answer my question; another murder charge will be added..."

"It is Hydrocodone®," says John.

"Julia, I will take Susan and start detoxing her. Don't worry, I think she will be OK," says Sam.

"Keep me posted, Sam," says Julia.

"Richard, please tell cadet Janis we have our guy and she can go back to her home. I will catch up with her later. I need you to bring the squad car over to Dickerson's Mortuary," says Julia.

"Dickerson's?" asks Richard.

"Yes, I will fill you in, later, at the office," says Julia.

THE DEBRIEF

J ulia, Richard and Bobbie discuss the series of events.

"Richard and Bobbie, please meet me in my office in fifteen minutes," says Julia.

"Betsy, please get Sam on the phone for me."

"Sam how is Susan?"

"She is conscious, and her vital signs have improved. I am going to take her to the hospital for a complete checkup. She will be all right, Julia."

"OK, guys, let's go over the series of events leading to those two in our jail. As you know, we decided to use the cadets, first, to lure the guy asking for dates, who happens to be Joe Lindsey, commonly called 'Joe the Ripper'. He had been released from the Jackson City Prison a couple weeks ago. Joe Lindsey was hired by John Dickerson to collect young females and kill them by causing them to overdose on Hydrocodone®. My original thoughts on the details of the dating and overdosing crimes were pretty accurate. In our plan, cadet Susan was propositioned by Joe Lindsey to a date in the strip club in a private viewing room. Susan pretended she had already shot up on opiates, which is what Joe Lindsey would have introduced to her, to lower her inhibitions. She acted in a way which did not demonstrate lowered inhibitions. It appears that Joe Lindsey was going to rape her, but was not able to because Susan would not give in. Joe Lindsey was hired by John Dickerson to deliver young female corpses to him," says Julia.

"I don't get the connection. Joe Lindsey rapes a woman, yet delivers them to John Dickerson as a corpse," says Bobbie.

"Joe Lindsey injected Susan with an opiate so as to cause an overdose leading to her death. Luckily for her, she faked she had previously shot up drugs, so Joe's injection was not enough to kill her," says Julia.

"Why did John Dickerson want young female corpses?" asks Richard.

"All I can tell you is when I entered Dickerson's examining room, John Dickerson was mounted on top of Susan and was about to penetrate her," says Julia.

"Holy shit! How gross is that? What the hell is wrong with that pervert?" asks Bobbie in disbelief.

"I am not sure. We will find out the whole story in court," says Julia.

LAURIE

Julia makes a phone call to Laurie Dickerson in hopes to help her understand what has happened with her husband, John Dickerson.

"Hello, Laurie Dickerson?" asks Julia.
 "Yes, this is Laurie. Is this Chief Lillus?"
 "Yes, could I come over to see you?"
 "Yes, please do. I am so confused."

JULIA DRIVES OVER TO THE MORTUARY TO MEET WITH LAURIE

"Hello, Chief Lillus."
 "Laurie, please call me Julia. How are you doing?"
 "I am so saddened by what I had seen John doing to that corpse. I

don't know what is the matter with him and why he would do such a thing. It is so sick, and to think I was having sex with a man who was having sex with dead women," says Laurie.

"I can't speak for him, but I believe he has Necrophilia. It is the desire to have sexual intercourse via vaginal penetration with dead corpses, and I think he has a higher than normal desire to have sex," says Julia.

"Yes, John does have a very unusually high desire to have sex. He pleaded with me to move our wedding up because he was having trouble with his urgency to have sex with me. I told him I would not enter into sexual intercourse before our marriage. After the wedding and before the reception, John had to have sex with me. He couldn't wait until later. Since the wedding, John has had me in bed at least twice a day. I have had to service his sexual desires whenever he requested it," says Laurie.

"Unfortunately, I don't have much to tell you because I have not completed questioning him and his accomplice. I was able to get from John, he was raped by his mother numerous times throughout his childhood into young adulthood. By doing these acts, she instilled in him that sex was the conduit to build his self-esteem. He said to me that he has a very hard time getting dates with females in order to fulfill his sexual desires to feed his self-esteem, so he decided to use female corpses because 'they' would not turn him down," says Julia.

"Oh, my Gosh! This is so complicated! I can't fathom this at all!" exclaims Laurie.

"Laurie, what are you going to do now? Is there any way I can help?" asks Julia.

"I am going to go back to my home and visit with my parents for some time. John's and my relationship is over as well as our marriage. I will need to pick up from there," says Laurie.

JOSEPH LINDSEY'S DAY IN COURT

T he Court House in Cloverville is bubbling with conversations of anger and indifference, on a warm summer day in June. Joseph Lindsey is in court with his lawyer.

"All rise! The court of the State vs. Lindsey is now in session, the Honorable Judge Newton is presiding."

"Please be seated," the bailiff announces.

"Mr. Blanding how does the defendant plead?" asks Judge Newton.

"The defendant pleads 'not guilty' your Honor."

"The defense calls Mr. Joseph Lindsey to the stand."

"Mr. Joseph Lindsey, do you solemnly swear to tell the truth and nothing but the truth so help you God?" asks the bailiff.

"Yes, I do," says Joseph Lindsey.

"Please be seated."

"Mr. Blanding, you may begin your line of questioning," says Judge Newton.

"Mr. Lindsey, describe to me what happened on the night of June 3rd."

"I went to the local strip club to find a date."

"Did you regularly frequent the strip club for dates?"

"Yes, and I also frequented bars in town and the surrounding counties."

"Did you find a date on the night of June 3rd at the local strip club, Mr. Lindsey?"

"Yes, I did."

"What was her name?"

"I don't know, I was just interested in dating her."

"Records show, Mr. Lindsey you and your date went to a private viewing room to share intimate relations. Is that so, Mr. Lindsey?"

"Yes, that was my intent, but she was high on something, so I figured the chances of intimacy with her was not going to be possible."

"Did you, then, leave the strip club, and how was your date when you left?"

"Yes, I cleared out of the club. She was unconscious from shooting up."

"Mr. Lindsey, I understand that a couple of months ago, you had finished your time in the Jackson City Prison?" asks attorney Blanding.

"Yes, that is correct."

"Mr. Lindsey, what were you doing time for at the prison?"

"Rape and suspected murder."

"Thank you, Mr. Lindsey."

"Mr. Dooley, would you like to like to question the defendant?" asks Judge Newton.

"Yes, your Honor," says attorney Dooley.

"Mr. Lindsey, you say you frequent strip clubs and bars to find dates. Is this your normal mode of trying to get 'laid'?"

"Objection! Your honor, the prosecution is insinuating my client's sole intent of dating is to have sexual relations with his date."

"Objection sustained."

"Mr. Dooley, please keep to the facts and do not lead the defendant," says Judge Newton.

"Mr. Lindsey, you have told us the girl you were trying to date was high on some drug?"

"Yes, she was. I think she was high on some opiate."

"Why would you say that, Mr. Lindsey? How did you come to that conclusion?"

"She told me she had shot up on opiates."

"You say that you tried or wanted to have sexual relations with her, but you either couldn't or did not want to?"

"Yes, normally a person, high on an opiates, will have lowered inhibitions, but her inhibitions were not lowered."

"If I understand you correctly, Mr. Lindsey, you did not want sexual relations with your date because her inhibitions were not lowered?"

"Yes, you are correct. I like women who have no inhibitions. You know, easier to get in their pants."

"Mr. Lindsey, the records show this young woman had a needle prick on her inner thigh. Do you think she injected the drug into herself at this site?"

"Yes, she probably did."

"The Coroner's report states the woman had a large amount of the drug in her bloodstream, enough to cause an overdose. How did your date function enough to go to the private viewing room, Mr. Lindsey?"

"I do not know. She walked with me to the private viewing room and she was conscious most of the time."

"Records show when the woman, your date, showed up at Dickerson's Mortuary, was presumed dead due to a large number of drugs in her system. How do you explain, Mr. Lindsey, she was conscious when you left her at the strip club and unconscious at the mortuary?"

"I don't know. Maybe she shot up after I left."

"Mr. Lindsay, a syringe with residue of an opiate drug was found in the private viewing room you and your date were occupying."

"See, I guess she did shoot up after I left."

"Mr. Lindsey, your fingerprints were on the syringe. Would you like to change your story?"

"OK, I gave her more drugs with the syringe."

"Where did you insert the syringe, Mr. Lindsey?"

"At her inner thigh."

"Why did you give her more drugs if she was already high, like you said she was?"

"I had to make sure she had an overdose."

"Why was it important to you she overdosed?"

"I was hired by the Dickerson Mortuary to drug young females to the point of overdose, so they could incur more dead bodies."

"Are you telling the court you purposely tried to cause the death of the victim, your date, to satisfy the needs of the Dickerson Mortuary?"

"Yes, I was hired to do just that. I was paid roughly four hundred dollars a head and could have sex with any of them I wanted."

"So, you initially gave drugs to lower your date's inhibitions, so she would allow you to have sex with her?"

"Objection, your Honor!" exclaims Attorney Blanding.

"The prosecution is insinuating my client gave the victim, his date, drugs to lower her inhibitions when he had clearly stated that she was high when he met her?"

"Objection sustained," says Judge Newton.

"Mr. Dooley, you will stick to the facts in this case and not make suppositions."

"Yes, your Honor," says attorney Dooley.

"Mr. Lindsey, how many women did Dickerson's Mortuary need?"

"I was asked to bring them as many females as I could."

"Did you bring the women physically to the mortuary?"

"No, my job was to search out young females in the age group from twenty to thirty years of age. I was to initially slip them drugs by way of a drink to get them high enough to lower their inhibitions, but not so high that I couldn't fuck them. When I was done, I was to give them more drugs by way of needle to cause an overdose. That is all. I have no idea how the females got to the mortuary."

"Mr. Lindsey, did you know that the overdoses you were administering caused death?"

"Yes, I knew the end result was death in order for the females to end up in the mortuary."

"So, how many women, say within the last three months have you had sex and caused an overdose of the drugs?"

"My guess is about ten to fifteen. I wasn't counting."

"With your employment with the Dickerson Mortuary, were you told why Mr. Dickerson needed the bodies of these females?"

"Initially, I was told he needed added bodies to boost his business. Later, I saw why he needed the bodies."

"Are you saying, Mr. Lindsey, the female bodies you caused death through overdosing with a drug for the Dickerson Mortuary was not to boost their business?"

"Right. He needed the bodies in order to fuck them."

The court roars with outbursts of disbelief.

"Order in this court," says Judge Newton. "There are to be no more outbursts in this court!"

"Mr. Lindsey, am I correct in saying you knew, when taking on the job with Dickerson's Mortuary, the women you dated would end in death?"

"Well, not really. I never knew if any of those women ended up dead. I just left them high and alive."

"But, you knew why Dickerson's Mortuary needed bodies and you were hired to get those bodies."

"I was tricked! Dickerson is the murderer!" exclaims Mr. Lindsey.

"No more questions, your Honor!"

"Mr. Blanding, do you have more questions for the defendant?" asks Judge Newton.

"No, your Honor, the defense rests."

"Court is adjourned and will convene tomorrow at noon with a verdict," says Judge Newton.

"All rise!" says the bailiff.

THE NEXT DAY, THE COURTROOM IS BUZZING WITH CONVERSATIONS OF
DISBELIEF AND DISDAIN FOR THE DEFENDANT AND THE DICKERSON
MORTUARY

"All rise! The court of the State vs. Lindsey is now in session. The Honorable Judge Newton presiding," the bailiff announces.

"We are here today to discover the verdict based on the facts leading to the most recent deaths of young females due to drug overdoses. Does the jury have a verdict?" asks Judge Newton.

"Yes, we do."

"Will the defendant please rise?" asks Judge Newton.

"Mr. Lindsey, the jury of your peers find you guilty of the rape and murder by way of purposely causing young females to overdose on a drug. Mr. Lindsey, you hired on with Dickerson's Mortuary knowing very well that you would supply them with corpses of young females. You also were desiring to rape those individuals before their death. Therefore, I sentence you to death by lethal injection in the Jackson City Prison. Court is adjourned," says Judge Newton.

"All rise!" exclaims the bailiff.

JOHN DICKERSON'S DAY IN COURT

The Court House in Cloverville is bubbling with conversations of disbelief and contempt, on a rainy day in July. John Dickerson is in court with his lawyer.

"All rise! The court of the State vs. Dickerson is now in session. The Honorable Judge Newton is presiding."

"Please be seated," the bailiff announces.

"Mr. Woodley how does the defendant plead?" asks Judge Newton.

"The defendant pleads 'not guilty' your Honor."

"The defense calls Mr. John Dickerson to the stand."

Mr. John Dickerson, do you solemnly swear to tell the truth and nothing but the truth so help you God?" asks the bailiff.

"Yes, I do," says John Dickerson.

"Please be seated."

"Mr. Dickerson, you are the owner and Mortician at Dickerson's Mortuary?" asks Mr. Woodley.

"Yes, I am."

"I understand you recently graduated from the Claire Bethany

School of Mortuary Sciences, and took over Mr. Liberty's Mortuary Services with a new business name?"

"Yes, that is correct."

"Records show you hired a Mr. Joseph Lindsey to help your business grow by searching out corpses for you?"

"Yes, that is correct."

"Describe to the court how Mr. Lindsey was to bring corpses to your business."

"I hired him to search out corpses in conjunction with the coroner to introduce my business services to the surrounding counties."

"Records show that you brought in young female corpses whose cause of death were from overdosing on drugs and that those female corpses were killed by your employee, Mr. Lindsey."

"Yes, that is correct, I did take in some female corpses due to overdosing of drugs, but I did not direct Mr. Lindsey to kill any of those females in order to fill my business with corpses."

"So, you didn't know your employee, Mr. Lindsey was killing females for you?"

"Absolutely not! I had just found out about it and I was about to fire him," says Mr. Dickerson.

"That is all the questions I have for Mr. Dickerson," says attorney Woodley.

"Mr. Paisley, you may question the defendant," says Judge Newton.

"Mr. Dickerson, please tell me what happened on the night of June 3rd."

"I was called by the local strip club to pick up a young female who they thought was dead in one of their viewing rooms. I thought it was weird for them to call a Mortuary and I thought maybe they mistook me for being a coroner or a doctor, you know, new business and all. So, I went to the strip club and posed as a doctor to pick up the female."

"Was the female dead as the strip club had informed you?"

"Yes, I was certain that she was dead. I took her to my mortuary and tried to contact the coroner. I did not have much luck, probably because it was much later in the night."

"Mr. Dickerson let us back up a bit. Did you know that the female you picked up at the strip club had been visited by your employee Mr. Lindsey?"

"No, I did not."

"So, you were certain the female was dead?"

"Yes."

"She was drugged to the point of overdose, and as a matter of fact, Mr. Lindsey has said that you hired him to drug young females to the point of overdose so that you would have a steady flow of corpses into your business," says attorney Paisley.

"As I said, I did not instruct him to kill in order to bring me corpses. I knew nothing of what he was doing."

"We have on record the strip club did not make any calls for a doctor to pick up a female from their place of business. They said a Doctor Fingerly showed up to pick up a female who overdosed on drugs. They said they did not know of any female overdose until the doctor arrived. Mr. Dickerson, did you pose as Doctor Fingerly?"

"Yes, and they must be mistaken because I did get a call from the strip club."

"Mr. Dickerson, we have witnesses who have said they saw you trying to have sexual intercourse with the female you brought from the strip club at your mortuary. Please explain this."

"I was starting to prepare the body. Sometimes I need to place myself in order to move body parts due to Rigor Mortis and it may appear I was trying to have relations with the body."

"Mr. Dickerson does one, in your profession, need to fill the vagina with lubricating gel and if so, what for?"

"No, there is no reason for that. There is nothing to be done with the female genitals when preparing a body."

"Why, then, did the female you brought from the strip club have lubricating gel in her vagina?"

"It probably came from initiating sexual relations with someone earlier. I don't know, I never need to look at that part of the body. There is no need. Most times, I never need to remove the underwear."

"Why, then, was the female you brought to your mortuary wearing no underwear; as a matter of fact, she was completely nude."

"As I recall, while preparing the body, I removed her outer clothing only to find she was wearing no bra or panties."

"That is all Mr. Dickerson."

"Please step down," says the bailiff.

"I would like to call Mrs. Laurie Dickerson to the stand," says attorney Paisley.

Mrs. Laurie Dickerson, do you solemnly swear to tell the truth and nothing but the truth so help you God?" asks the bailiff.

"Yes, I do," says Laurie Dickerson.

"Please be seated."

"Mrs. Dickerson how long have you and Mr. Dickerson been married?" asks attorney Paisley.

"We have only been married for a couple months."

"During the time with Mr. Dickerson, did you know your husband was taking in a lot of corpses; female corpses?"

"Yes, I did. He told me he had hired a guy to help advertise the business to bring in clients to build the business."

"Mrs. Dickerson, did you suspect or feel anything peculiar about your relationship with your husband?"

"Not, but he does have a huge appetite for sex, I must say."

"How so, Mrs. Dickerson?"

"Well, he desires to have sexual intercourse with me at least two times a day. It kind of wears me out."

"Mrs. Dickerson, on the night of June 3rd explain what happened."

"I went to bed early because I was tired. John was not ready for bed at the time and had just come back from the store because he was low on alcohol for which he uses to sanitize. He told me he would join me soon. I was awakened by a knock on the door. I got up and found Mr. Lindsey, John's employee, at the door and insisted he see John. I tried to table it to the next day because it was so late, but he insisted he talk to John. So, I took him down to John's preparing room and knocked on the door to tell John Mr. Lindsey was to talk to him. I opened the door and oh......!"

"Go ahead, Mrs. Dickerson. What did you see?"

"There was a young female body on the preparing table and she was nude. John was up on the table between her legs and looked like he was going to penetrate her."

"Why do you say that, Mrs. Dickerson?"

"Well, he had his pants unzipped and his penis was out and erect ready to penetrate her."

"What happened next?"

"Chief Lillus arrived and arrested both John and Mr. Lindsey."

"That is all the questions the prosecution has," says attorney Paisley.

"Mr. Woodley, do you have questions for the witness?" asks Judge Newton.

"No, your Honor, the defense rests," says attorney Woodley.

"Your Honor, I would like to call Mr. John Dickerson to the stand," says attorney Paisley.

"May I remind you, Mr. Dickerson, you are still under oath," says Judge Newton.

"Yes, your Honor," says John Dickerson.

"Mr. Dickerson, it is on record you suffer from Necrophilia, or Intense Sexual Chemistry with the dead."

"Yes, it is what they say, but I do have a huge sexual appetite, as my wife has testified."

"So, you were institutionalized for a while in your teenage years?"

"Yes, that is true, but I have since been cured."

"Yet you say you have a huge sexual appetite."

"I am a typical male with an unusual amount of testosterone, that is all."

"Mr. Dickerson, on the night of June 3rd was it your intention to have sexual relations with that young girl on your preparing table?"

"I really thought about it. She was so beautiful. I was ready too, but felt I needed to go to my bedroom and work it out with my wife."

"Mr. Dickerson were you having sexual relations with the female corpses you brought into your mortuary?"

"Absolutely not! What kind of animal do you think I am?"

"Let me tell you what the records show. It was found that the lubricant found in the female body's vagina matched the vaginal lubricant you have stored in your cabinet. If the vagina is not a part of the body preparation, then why was lubricant found in her vagina and why do you have bottles of vaginal lubricant stocked in your cabinet? A turkey baster was found with traces of that same lubricant and pubic hair was also found on it. DNA testing was done on the turkey baster and there were over twenty different DNA strains along with your DNA. It appears that you used the turkey baster to inject vaginal lubricant into many different female's vaginas, so you could insert your penis. You, sir, were having sexual intercourse with female corpses."

"Objection!" exclaims attorney Woodley.

"Objection overruled," says Judge Newton. "Continue, Mr. Paisley."

"Mr. Dickerson, it stands to reason you were collecting young female corpses by way of your hired employee Mr. Lindsey and having sexual relations with them to feed your zest for Necrophilia. It appears you are not cured."

"I didn't kill those girls! Joseph Lindsey killed those girls!" exclaims John Dickerson.

"How do you know Mr. Joseph Lindsey killed all those girls? We were exploring the facts of only one female here; the one you were seen mounting. Now you are talking about more girls being murdered? How do you know that Mr. Dickerson?"

"Objection!" exclaimed attorney Woodley.

"I, I…was just suggesting he did it! Not that I did it! It is just a guess!"

"No! No, Mr. Dickerson! You hired Mr. Joseph Lindsey to kill young female girls so that you could have them to yourself, in your mortuary, to have sexual relations with them, didn't you Mr. Dickerson?"

"Objection!" exclaims attorney Woodley, again.

"No! No! I didn't kill them! They were dead when I got them. What is wrong with having sexual intercourse with dead female girls?

It wasn't like I was raping them! They didn't complain! They wanted it!" exclaims Mr. John Dickerson.

"Why, Mr. Dickerson, do you have a running stock of opiate drugs? Why do corpses need those?"

"We have to get their inhibitions down. I can only fuck them if their inhibitions are down. No, they won't go on a date with me without those drugs. No, they won't have sex with me unless they are dead. No, I had to have them killed, so I could fuck them. Yes, I fucked them. I killed them, so I could fuck them. I must lubricate their vaginas. Oh, I must keep them warm. I can't let Rigor Mortis set in. No, I mustn't. Their nipples were so erect, when I sucked on them, even when they were dead. Oh, you must come to Dickerson's Mortuary. I will take care of your needs. Sweetheart, you will love this….," babbles Mr. John Dickerson.

"Your Honor, I have no more questions," says attorney Paisley.

"Guards, please take Mr. Dickerson to the detainment room," says Judge Newton.

"I killed them; I fucked them! They wanted it! I fucked them…. I fucked them…," babbles Mr. John Dickerson as he is led from the courtroom.

"Court is adjourned and will convene tomorrow at noon with a verdict," says Judge Newton.

"All rise!" says the bailiff.

OUTSIDE THE COURTHOUSE JULIA ENTERS INTO CONVERSATION WITH
LAURIE DICKERSON

"Oh, my dear, I cannot believe what I just heard. He is sick! That man is sick and crazy! I married a crazy man," she wales while crying.

"Laurie, please, come with me," says Julia Lillus.

"I just don't know what to think. I was having intimately relations with a man who was fucking dead girls! Who the hell does those things?" asks Laurie Dickerson.

"Laurie, John is sick and is suffering from Intense Sexual Chemistry. He learned the only method to maintain self-esteem was to have sexual relations with a female; his mother years ago. When he couldn't get his intense desires satisfied, he pursued the only females that would allow his acts of intense sexual activity; dead corpses. He tried to get satisfaction through you, but you couldn't give him enough," says Julia.

"Julia, I gave him as much sex as he desired. I wore myself out for him to a point where I no longer enjoyed sexual intercourse."

"It wasn't enough. He needed the interaction in an almost continuous fashion. Somehow in his childhood, his 'wires' got crossed in his brain resulting with his obsession. The records show he was very close to his mother and she lured him to having sexual relations with her at such an early age; his developmental years. He was doomed," says Julia.

"What will happen to him now, Julia?"

"I am not sure, but he will probably spend the rest of his life in a mental institution. He cracked in the courtroom. It will probably be next to impossible to bring him back for any useful therapy," says Julia.

"I do not know what to do. In a way, I still love John. I even think I love him more because of the discovery of his sickness. I do feel sorry for him," Laurie Dickerson cries as she hugs Julia.

"Laurie, I can relate to you. I have had a similar situation with my late husband. He was a very sick man. I loved him so much and I still do even in his death. I will always love him just like you will always love John."

"How do you cope, Julia?"

"Some days I do not cope, but I just keep moving forward and try to fill my life with positive people who love me and whom I love. The pain I feel emotionally for my late husband never leaves me."

"I don't know if I can do that. I don't know anyone here and no one knows me."

"Laurie, why don't you stay with me for a while. I have a small apartment I share with a wonderful mom and her daughter and I am sure we can make room for you. Stay as long as you like."

"Thank you, Julia. I will consider it, but I think I will go and visit with my parents for a while."

"OK, just keep in touch with me. Call me anytime you want to talk, and my home is always open for you."

"Thank you so much, Julia. You are such a sweet woman and I now know I have at least one person I love."

"And one person who loves you!" exclaims Julia.

THE HEARTBREAKING VERDICT

T he Court House in Cloverville is quiet; so quiet one could hear
a pin drop on a cloudy and cool afternoon in July. John
Dickerson is in court with his lawyer and shows signs of babbling to
himself with a blank stare off into the distance.

"All rise! The court of the State vs. Dickerson is now in session. The
Honorable Judge Newton is presiding."

"Please be seated," the bailiff announces.

"Mr. Woodley, would you please help Mr. John Dickerson to
stand?" asks Judge Newton.

"Mr. Dickerson, please try to look at me while I talk to you. Do
you understand me?" asks Judge Newton.

John Dickerson continues to stare in the direction of the Judge,
but his stare 'goes through the Judges face', and ends somewhere on
the wall behind.

"Mr. Dickerson, the jury of your peers has found you guilty of a
conspiracy to murder young female women so as to feed your intense
zest for sexual intimacy with them. You are also found guilty of raping

those women by having sexual intercourse with them without their consent. It is also known you suffer from Necrophilia."

"Therefore, Mr. Dickerson, I sentence you to serve the rest of your life in the Marcy State Institute for the Mentally Impaired where your care will address your sickness. You will have limited visitation with your wife. Your sentence in no way releases you from the conviction of murder and rape. If you are to be cured while at the Institution, you will complete the remainder of your sentence in the Jackson City Prison. Court is adjourned," says Judge Newton.

"All rise!" says the bailiff.

BACK AT THE POLICE DEPARTMENT

Back at the office, Julia explains the turn of events to Richard and Bobbie. Richard and Bobbie take the opportunity to continue their love affair.

"Julia, how did the court case involving John Dickerson turn out? We heard he cracked at the end," says Bobbie.

"It was a very spooky case and very disturbing. It is hard for me to grasp, even he being mentally sick; having sexual relations with corpses was desired? It makes me sick just thinking about it. I feel so sorry for his wife, Laurie. The poor woman tried to satisfy his sexual prowess to the point of wearing herself out."

"I can kind of relate to that," says Bobbie as she looks over at Richard.

"What? Why you are looking at me, Bobbie?" asks Richard.

"You know why, Richard."

"I offered for her to stay with me and Nicole for a while," says Julia.

"Julia, you have such a heart of gold!"

"Well, Bobbie, I can relate to her. Even though her husband is sick; masterminded and carried out such sinister acts, she still loves him. I bet she will always love him, just like I will never stop loving Tim, no matter what he did."

"That is exactly what I mean, Julia. You have such a love for humanity. I envy you."

"Ok, Richard, something just crossed my mind. If you didn't have me, would you revert to satisfying yourself with female corpses?" asks Bobbie.

"What? Why in hell would you even think of that?"

"Well, Richard, you cannot seem to be able to keep your hands off of me. I was just wondering what you would do if I weren't around."

"I would cope. I could deal with it. I am sure."

"I am not sure you could cope at all! How would you satisfy your intense desire for sex?"

"I could do it. I would have to do it."

"Ok, let's take a test. For the next week; oh, that will certainly not work. For the next two days you are not to touch me, and you absolutely cannot have sex with me," states Bobbie.

"Oh, this is starting to sound interesting," says Julia.

"I can do it, Bobbie. I know I could do it for a week," says Richard.

"Yeah, sure Richard!" exclaims Bobbie.

"Ok, we will do another test right now."

"Go ahead Bobbie; you will lose," says Richard.

"Julia, who do you think will win in this test?" asks Bobbie.

"It is tough to say, but if I were to guess as to what I think the test will involve, I surely feel Richard will lose."

"Julia, you fail me! You two women don't really know me," responds Richard.

"Richard, are you ready for this test?" asks Bobbie.

"Yes, Bobbie, bring it on."

"Wait a minute, Bobbie. What the hell are you doing?"

"Did I just witness you dropping your skirt? Oh, no, now you are unbuttoning your blouse? What? That teddy is all lace? Oh my God! Now what? Taking off your shoes? No, Bobbie! No, Bobbie! Oh, hell, you just have to bend over to take your shoes off with your ass towards me? This is totally not fair!"

"Richard, it looks like you are losing!"

"What do you mean, Bobbie?"

"Take a look at your crotch. Do I see 'one-eyed willy' poking your pants?"

"Sorry, guys, I have some paperwork to do," says Julia.

"Bobbie, you are right. I couldn't cope without you. I can't lose you."

"Julia, please don't enter the break-room for a while and you might want to turn your radio on for a bit," says Richard.

"Bobbie, it is time to test you. Let's see how long it takes you to 'cum'. I bet it won't take too long. So, please sweetheart, remove the teddy and bend over the back of the couch."

AFTER THE QUICKIE

Richard fails Bobbie's test but the ladies feel Richard actually won.

"Richard, once my heartbeat returns to normal, I will see you home. I will make your dinner when I get there."

"Bobbie, it is my treat tonight! I am making dinner and I will take care of dessert, too. See you soon, sweetheart," says Richard.

"Ok, honey, but I think I have had enough 'dessert' for one day. Give me a kiss!"

"Julia, I think I cheated a bit with the test for Richard. I enticed him with my teddy," says Bobbie with a grin on her face.

"You did more than that! You undressed in front of him. I was concerned you had nothing under your clothes," says Julia.

"Oh, usually I don't, but I did have intentions of seducing him sometime today. He has been working so hard lately. Besides, I like to tease him. I can't give him the whole 'picture' all at once."

"It appears he didn't care. As a matter of fact, I would guess it turned out just how he wanted it, and he might have even been putting you on just to get where he wanted with you," says Julia.

"Yeah, he got his way, didn't he? Actually, I am glad it turned out the way it did. I couldn't cope without him either," says Bobbie.

"You two are perfect for each other. I am so happy to see your healthy relationship. But I am concerned I might end up being a godmother for a whole passel of children with the last name of Peltz," says Julia.

"Well, Julia, do you really think we are stopping at just one child?"

"Watching you two, well, no, I believe you aren't," says Julia.

AMANDA ALEXANDRIA

J ulia is sifting papers at her desk as her office phone rings.

"Yes, Betsy, what is it?" asks Julia.

"There is a young woman out here who is looking to talk to you."

"Ok Betsy, send her into my office. Thanks."

"Hello? How may I help you?" asks Julia.

"Hi, my name is Amanda Alexandria. I was sent here by the City Council. They had said you were looking for another deputy."

"Oh yes, I am looking for a deputy, but I told them I needed a deputy with a specialty in Forensics. My name is Julia Lillus. I am the Chief for this Department. It is nice to meet you, Amanda."

"I come from downstate, the Queens to be exact, and my job was in Forensics. I held that position for five years."

"What brings you to our little town?" asks Julia.

"Actually, I was getting burned out. I am looking for a slower pace than what I had in the City."

"We certainly have a slower pace, here in Harford, but I must warn you we get some very peculiar cases here."

"Oh, I am not afraid of peculiar cases. As a matter of fact, I thrive on them," says Amanda.

"I have two very experienced deputies. Richard and Bobbie are like family to me. If I were to bring you into our department, I would expect you to not enter into competition with them. They are very good in what they do; but we are lacking in the Forensic Sciences. Adding you to this department would be for the Forensics Sciences. We need a Forensics Lab here."

"I understand perfectly, Chief Lillus. I do not believe in competing in the workplace and my wish is to be the Forensics asset to your department."

"Great! We will benefit having you part of the team. When will you be able to start?" asks Julia.

"I will need to obtain an apartment and move my belongings. I am hoping in about two weeks," says Amanda.

"Ok, why don't you start the first of next month. It will give you three weeks to get settled and give me time to get you set up with an office," says Julia.

"That will be fine," says Amanda.

"Amanda, I have always dreamed of having a small Forensics Lab in our Department. The City Council has given me the green light. Do you think you can set a Lab up for us?"

"I sure can," answers Amanda.

"It will be your Lab and an extension to your office. The City has given me a modest budget of ten thousand dollars for this Lab. Your first assignment will be for you to order the lab instruments you need. I will take care of the construction of the Lab area, but I will need a rough sketch of how you would like it laid out."

"Super! No problem! I am so excited! I will stay within the budget. Thank you so much, Chief Lillus."

"In our office, we go by names and are not very formal. Please call me Julia. Oh, and the City pays well. When you come in, I will introduce you to Bobbie and Richard. You will love them. They are husband and wife; they are really into each other, so don't be surprised if you happen to see some heavy flirting going on between the two of them."

"I love seeing healthy legitimate relationships," says Amanda.

THE INTRODUCTION

J ulia announces to Richard and Bobbie of Amanda Alexandria's
start of her career at the Harford Police Department.

"Bobbie and Richard, I have hired a Forensic Deputy. She will be
starting in three weeks," says Julia.

"We have needed one of those for such a long time. Maybe now,
we can get into some pretty deep cases outside our little town," says
Bobbie.

"The City Council has given us enough of a budget to build a small
Forensic Lab, too. Her Lab and office will be over here in this section.
I want you both to know she will be exclusive to Forensics. I mean,
your responsibilities will not change, and she will not interfere with
your work. I talked to her about this and she doesn't want to do what
you do. She is a kind of scientist in Forensics and she is more than
happy to stick with that," says Julia.

"Julia, how old is this girl or woman?" asks Richard.

"Richard, you know I am not allowed to ask that, but I would guess
mid-twenties," says Julia.

"Richard, why do you need to know her age?" asks Bobbie.

"The younger they are, the more they think they know it all!" exclaims Richard.

"There will be nothing like that, Richard. She is definitely not like that at all," says Julia.

THREE WEEKS LATER, IT IS AMANDA ALEXANDRIA'S FIRST DAY AY THE HARFORD POLICE DEPARTMENT

"Amanda, this is Bobbie and Richard Peltz. Bobbie and Richard, this is Amanda Alexandria. She comes from downstate and she is quite an expert in Forensics. Amanda, Bobbie and Richard have been with this Department for quite a while and they bring expertise to this Department matched by no one."

"It is very nice to meet you, Amanda," says Bobbie.

"Yes, it is my pleasure to have you as part of our Department," says Richard.

"Richard, come into my office. I have to go over a few things before we get started today," says Bobbie.

"Richard, do you think Amanda is attractive? Is she pretty?" asks Bobbie.

"Bobbie, do I feel a bit of jealousy here? To answer your question, I do see Amanda as an attractive woman, but she is no match for you," says Richard.

"I am not jealous, Richard. I was just wondering."

"Sweetheart, you are and always will be the only woman for me. I love you so much, Bobbie. There is no woman in this world who could replace you. You are beautiful and so enticing to me. You also bring so much stability to our relationship. We have such a beautiful daughter that only you could have given to us. May I also add, I am quite fond of your…," says Richard as he gestures toward Bobbie's thighs.

"Richard!"

"Come over here, honey. I want to give you a deep and passionate kiss. Bobbie, dear, I think little Julia needs a sister or brother. Maybe sometime?"

"I have a feeling he or she will come sooner than later. Shall we work on it tonight?" asks Bobbie.

"I am 'up' for it, if you know what I mean."

"'One Eyed Willie' rises again?" asks Bobbie.

NEW CLOWN IN TOWN

A stranger has come to Harford and frequents the Children's Hospital in Syracuse as a clown. There is a discussion starting at the Police Department.

"Hey, Julia, did you hear about the clown visiting the Syracuse area Children's Hospitals?" asks Amanda.

"Yes, I heard about the clown. Supposedly the clown is taking it upon himself to bring joy to the children in the area hospitals."

"I also heard he frequents the city park on pleasant-weather days doing tricks for children," says Amanda.

"Guess what else is happening in our little city of Harford?" asks Bobbie.

"Hopefully something good, I am getting worn out on those strange cases we have had lately," says Julia.

"We are going to have a Children's Beauty Pageant," says Bobbie.

"I worry about those Pageants. They tend to draw pedophiles," says Julia.

"Let's go over the area pedophile listing and get reacquainted with their photos. We will have to be on the look-out when the day of the Pageant arrives," says Bobbie.

"I am going to pay a visit at one of the hospitals and introduce myself to the clown and get some information from him. I get skeptical when certain people like that suddenly show up in our area," says Julia.

"Hey, maybe you can take little Julia Ann with you. She would love to see the clown," says Bobbie.

"Sure, I would love too," says Julia.

JULIA INTRODUCES HERSELF TO THE CLOWN

J ulia takes a trip over to Richard and Bobbie's home to pick up little Julia Ann.

"Julia Ann, how would you like to go with me and see a clown at the hospital?" asks Julia.

"Hee Hee, a clone; I see clone," Julia Ann chuckles.

"Julia Ann, it is pronounced 'clown'; can you say it? Look at me as I say it. See my mouth open as I say, 'clown' and how my lips open and….That's OK, Julia Ann, you will get it in time. I shouldn't expect so much from a little tyke who just started to formulate words. Ok, let's get you dressed so you can see the clown. What would you like to wear on this beautiful warm day, Julia Ann? The red skirt and the monkey shirt? I love that little monkey on your shirt. Is he the same stuffed monkey doll you have on your bed?"

"His name is 'shecoo'," says Julia Ann.

"Oh, I think you mean, 'Chico'," says Julia.

JULIA AND JULIA ANN DRIVE TO THE HOSPITAL TO MEET THE CLOWN

"Excuse me, Mr. Clown. My name is Julia Lillus and I am the Police Chief for the Harford Police Department and this is my goddaughter, Julia Ann," says Julia.

"Oh, such a cutie! Julia Ann, watch me while I make a puppy dog for you out of these balloons," says the clown.

"Mr. Clown, can we go over to the break room? I would like to get to know the real you. It is my job to welcome newcomers in Harford," says Julia.

"Julia Ann, I will get you an ice cream cone and you can sit next to me and play with your puppy dog balloon while I talk to Mr. Clown, OK?" Mr. Clown, or should I….."

"You can call me Judd Finney. It is my name," says the clown.

"Mr. Finney, what brings you to our area?"

"I am a retired school teacher and I love to bring smiles to children. I always did while I was actively teaching."

"What school were you actively teaching?"

"I was teaching at the Gloversville Elementary up north. I was a Physical Education teacher."

"What brings you here as a clown?"

"I want to continue to bring smiles to children in my retirement years, so I feel being dressed up as a clown and visiting children at the area hospitals and the parks, on nice weather days, will do just that."

"Mr. Finney, are you married or have any children?"

"No, I never married, and do not have any children. Somedays I wish that I had married and had children, but I can be with as many children as I want now."

"Where are you staying, Mr. Finney?"

"I have an apartment in Gloversville at the moment, but my plan is to secure a house somewhere close to this area and the hospitals. I am thinking the Dewitt area would be nice for me to settle in."

"Mr. Finney, I am assuming you do the clown act for free? Do you have another job?"

"No, I do not at the moment. I do have a rather generous retirement fund I draw from. It should be sufficient for now."

"What kind of acts do you perform for the children?"

"No, Julia Ann, Mr. Clown already made you a balloon puppy."

"It's OK. Julia Ann, would you like me to make you a bouquet of flowers?" asks Mr. Finney.

Julia Ann shakes her head in agreement and says, "fowers; petty fowers."

"Here you go, Julia Ann; a bouquet of pretty flowers."

"How did you do that," asks Julia.

"Oh, just a little trick 'up my sleeve'. I can't divulge to you my tricks. It would be no fun for you adults with children," says Mr. Finney.

"Well, Mr. Finney, it is nice meeting you and thanks for adding entertainment for little Julia Ann. I am sure I will see you around town," says Julia.

"My pleasure, Chief Lillus."

"Just call me Julia. I don't believe in such formalities."

"Juwia, Juwia," says Julia Ann.

"Julia Ann, you call me 'auntie' OK?" says Julia with a little chuckle.

LAUGHTER IS THE BEST MEDICINE

J ulia and Julia Ann return to the office to reunite Julia Ann with
her mother.

"Julia and little Julia Ann! So how was your visit with the clown?" asks
Bobbie.

"Juwia, Juwia"

"What is that? What is she saying?" asks Bobbie.

"Oh, I told the clown he didn't need to be so formal and he could
call me by my name and this little gal picked up on it and won't stop
saying it. It is funny how she cannot pronounce it correctly," Julia
laughs.

"Julia Ann, honey, this is 'auntie'," says Bobbie.

"Juwia, Juwia, Juwia!"

"No, Julia Ann, this is 'auntie'. Oh, and look at your puppy and the
bouquet of flowers!" exclaims Bobbie.

"Clone gave me poopy."

Laughing hysterically, Bobbie says, "No honey, it is pronounced
'clown' and this is a 'puppy'."

"Poopy. Fower for mommy."

"This little gal just cracks me up! She is forever keeping me and Richard in stitches. We try not to laugh in front of her, but sometimes we can't help it," says Bobbie.

"She definitely is a bundle of joy!" exclaims Julia.

"Julia Ann, go over there and show your puppy balloon to all of your stuffed animals. Julia, it is such a nice gesture for you to allow an area in our office for Julia Ann to play."

"Bobbie, I wouldn't have it any other way. I love children as much as you and Richard. One of these days I am going to kidnap little Julia Ann."

"Ok, Juwia," says Bobbie as they both burst out in laughter.

"Let me tell you about my interview with the clown. He is a retired school teacher from the Gloversville Elementary School and says he likes to make children laugh. He will be staying, eventually here, in this area. He is looking in the Dewitt area for a home. His name is Judd Finney. Does that ring any bells for you?" asks Julia.

"No, do you have a funny feeling about him, Julia?" asks Bobbie.

"No, not really, I am just cautious of strangers coming to town and especially a clown. We don't see them very often."

"You got that right! Well, what is on tap for today, Julia?"

"Nothing at the moment. If you and Julia Ann want to go home, it will be OK with me. I can call you if I need you for anything. Besides, Richard's shift will be starting in a couple of hours. Go home and have fun with Julia Ann," suggests Julia.

LANDING A HOME FOR THE CLOWN

M r. Finney meets with a realtor for the possibility of finding a home.

"Mr. Finney, this is a very nice ranch home for a single guy. It is a two bedroom one and a half bath with a converted garage to a family room. It is nice and cozy, nestled behind the hedgerow of pines, blocking out the traffic noise. You will be on a major roadway leading to Manlius and the Dewitt area. There are many retails stores in the area; many restaurants and a mall."

"Where does this stairway lead?"

"Oh, these stairs lead down to the basement. I forgot to mention the partitioned room under the, what used to be garage. They have shored up the ceiling with steel beams to support the concrete floor above. That area would make a great office for you, or even a guest bedroom for lengthy stays. There is a bathroom within the room. My guess is the past owners must have had an in-law staying with them and that was their room; it is well furnished."

"How much is the asking price?" asks Judd Finney.

"Ninety-thousand which includes a home warranty for ten years. The warranty, in itself, is worth almost half of the cost. The previous owners want to be sure that whoever purchases this house will be happy and the house warranty covers major issues that might occur."

"Let's draw up the required paperwork. When will the closing be?" asks Judd Finney.

"Let's go to my office. We will get all of that squared up. I am guessing, in that you are paying cash, the closing will be by the end of the month."

FURNISHING THE HOME

A fter the purchase of his home, Mr. Finney hires a an interior decorator to furnish the home before he moves into it.

"Hello, Mr. Finney?"

"Yes, I am Judd Finney."

"I am answering the ad you had in the paper for a painter and home decorator."

"Oh yes, I am looking to have my home completely repainted with more bright colors. The previous owners must have taken a liking to living in darkness."

"Yes, I can see that! What colors do you have in mind?"

"I am looking for a beige type paint for the living areas and an off-white for the bedrooms. There is a room in the basement I would like painted with a bright happy color. Maybe paint some balloons on the walls, etc. You see, I am a clown for the local hospitals and I am going to use the room as my make-up and dressing room. The colors and happy things painted on the walls will aid in preparing the needed mood for visiting the children," says Judd Finney.

"No problem, I will get the supplies I need and start tomorrow afternoon if it works for you?"

"Yes, it will be a good time for I will be at the hospital visiting the children. There is a key to the door under the mat at the back door," says Judd Finney.

EMERGENCY MEETING AT THE POLICE DEPARTMENT

I ssues, once again, begin to ramp-up at the Harford Police Department.

"Bobbie and Richard, please come into my office immediately! I just received a call from a desperate mother stating her child is missing. She said she and her daughter were in the park. She went to get ice cream at the stand and when she turned around to give the ice cream cone to her daughter, she was not at her side," says Julia.

"She must have wandered off? How long ago did you get the call?" asks Bobbie.

"She called about a half hour ago. What is it Betsy?"

"Chief Lillus, a woman is out here crying and wants to see you immediately."

"Please send her in. Hello, ma'am, what can we do for you?" asks Julia.

"I called about forty minutes ago about my missing daughter. I cannot find her anywhere," cries the woman.

"Tell me; was your daughter at your side at all times going to the ice cream stand?"

"Yes, she was at my side, and after I turned to tell Cindy we would have to wait a minute for the chocolate ice cream, she was gone."

"You didn't see her anywhere?"

"No, I turned around to tell her and she had vanished like she never was there."

"Ma'am, how old is your daughter and what does she look like?" asks Bobbie.

"Her name is Cindy and she is eleven years old. She has blonde hair, long, and freckles across the bridge of her nose. She has blue eyes and olive skin tones and is wearing shorts and a halter type top."

"Was there anyone in the park that she may have known? Did you go to the park with Cindy alone?" asks Julia.

"There were lots of kids in the park her age and probably some of her friends, but she and I did not converse with any one of them and Cindy was by my side at all times. She may look older than eleven, but she is quite shy and doesn't mix well with kids her age."

"Mrs....?" asks Julia.

"My name is Ellie, Ellie Myers."

"Mrs. Myers, was there anything peculiar or different about your visit to the park? Was there anything which might have drawn Cindy's attention away from you?" asks Richard.

"No, not that I know of, it just was a busy day at the park; more than usual, but you know, with the good weather, I guess everyone was out enjoying it. I am worried about Cindy. I need to find her! Can you help me please?" Mrs. Myers says as she bursts into tears.

"Bobbie, will you take Mrs. Myers to her home and stay with her?" asks Julia.

"Yes, Mrs. Myers, let me take you home. I will stay with you for a while."

"Richard, get over to the park and ask questions. Survey the area to see if anything strange is going on over there. Amanda, I am going to step out and interview some parents who had or have children at the park," says Julia.

"OK, I will wait your return," says Amanda.

THE CLOWN IN THE PARK

C indy and her mother decide to enjoy the beautiful weather and
visit he Community Park.

"Cindy, would you like an ice cream cone to finish our day in the
park?" asks Ellie Myers.

"Yes, mommy, I would. Can we go over and see the clown? He is
making balloon animals and passing them out to the little kids. He is
making paper flower bouquets for the older ones and I would like to
get one for you, mommy," says Cindy.

"Well, we will see. It looks like he is done for today. He is packing
up his things and all of the kids have left."

"Let's hurry up at the ice cream stand before the clown leaves the
park. Oh, look, he has a cute puppy with him. I love puppies, mommy.
I hope he will let me pet the puppy. Hurry, mommy, let's run over to
the ice cream stand!"

"Maybe you don't want ice cream, Cindy?"

"Oh, yes , I do, mommy."

Cindy and her mother stroll over to the ice cream stand

"Hello, I would like a cone with a double dip. One is to be vanilla and the other chocolate. Please put sprinkles on it, too," says Ellie.

As Ellie is talking to the person at the park ice cream shop and ordering the ice cream cone for Cindy, the clown gets the attention of Cindy and motions to her to come over to him. Cindy's eyes light up when she sees the puppy in his arms. As the clown continues to motion to Cindy, she walks over to him and he offers to allow her to pet the puppy.

"I am sorry miss, but I will need to open a new bucket of chocolate. It will not take too long, I promise," says the girl at the ice cream shop.

"That is OK, I will wait."

"Cindy, it will not take much longer," says Ellie as she turns around to tell Cindy.

"Cindy, Cindy! Where are you Cindy?"

Ellie looks around and sees the clown across the pathway.

"Mr. Clown, have you seen my daughter, Cindy?" asks Ellie. The clown motions to her with his hands in the air and nods his head indicating a 'no'. She takes a hurried walk around the area of the ice cream shop and doesn't see her daughter anywhere.

THE INVITE

C indy walks quickly over to the clown as he motions to her.

As the clown releases the puppy into Cindy's arms, he motions to her indicating he has more puppies in the back of his van. He opens the doors and Cindy sees a couple other puppy dogs. Each one of the puppies run to the doorway with their tales wagging and jump up on Cindy as she gazes into the van. The clown motions to her to get closer so she can release the puppy in her arms and pet the other two. The clown lifts Cindy up into the van so she can pet the puppies. The clown immediately shuts the van doors with Cindy trapped inside. Cindy starts to holler and bang on the doors.

"Mr. Clown, please open the doors. I need to go get my ice cream cone," says Cindy. She continues to holler and bang on the van doors. Suddenly, the van starts to move, and Cindy begins to cry.

The van comes to a stop after a while and a door to the van begins to open.

"Mr. Clown, why did you lock me in here? Help me! Can anyone hear me?" cries Cindy.

"No one can hear you darling. The walls and doors are padded. No one will hear you."

"Who are you? Why did you bring me here? What are you going to do to me?"

"I am not going to do anything to you. I am a clown. I don't hurt children. So, what is your name, honey?"

"My name is Cindy and I want to go home to my mommy."

"I will bring you back to your mommy after the party."

"What party?" asks Cindy.

"I am having a clown party and all of the kids are invited."

"Where are the kids?"

"They are already at the party and I am taking you to them. We will have fun and after the party, I will bring you all back to your homes."

"How do you know where I live?" asks Cindy

THE PARTY

Judd Finney leads Cindy to the basement stairs in his home.

"Where are we?" asks Cindy.

"We are at the party. All of the kids are down there already having fun with the music and games. You can bring the puppies with you. They will follow."

Cindy follows the clown down the stairs as the music she hears is getting louder.

"Here, Cindy, beyond this door is the party. Go ahead and go in and join the kids. I will be back in a minute."

Cindy enters the room and immediately notices there are no kids having a party. There is a record player playing the music. Just as she turns around to leave the room, the door slams shut, and she hears the clown going back up the stairs. She tries to open the door, but realizes it is locked. She turns around and looks at the room. The walls are a bright pink with balloons painted on them. There is a canopy bed with plush looking pink sheets and bedspread. The dresser has two dolls sitting upon it and there are some other toys in a box in the corner. Around the pillows on the bed sits a couple of stuffed bear dolls. Cindy walks over to the dresser and pulls one of the drawers open. She sees various articles of clothes; dresses, underwear and socks, all of which are very rich looking.

Suddenly, the door to the room in the basement is unlocked and opens. The clown enters the room.

"You really aren't a clown, are you mister!"

"Yes, I am. Don't I look like a clown?"

"Clowns don't steal children and lock them in a room," says Cindy.

"Well, darling, I have everything you will need right here in this room."

"I don't want to be here. I want to go home to my mommy."

"I can't do that, honey. I need you to stay here with me. This is your bedroom now. There is a bathroom over there and I have furnished everything for you. I have toys for you and some dolls over there."

"I don't want any of that! I want to go home."

"I will allow the puppies to stay with you to keep you company. Now, why don't you clean up a bit. I would like you to put on this outfit after you clean up. I will bring your dinner to you in about a half hour."

"I don't want to wear these clothes. I want my own clothes."

"Well, that can't happen. Now go into the bathroom and strip down your clothes. Hand them out to me and I will hand you the outfit. I want you to look pretty for dinner. I will wash your clothes for you."

"I won't do that!" exclaims Cindy, as she starts to cry.

"If you want me to bring you back to your mommy after the party, you had better follow what I tell you. Now, get into the bathroom and do what I say!"

Cindy reluctantly walks into the bathroom because she wants to go back to her home and he promises to bring her back.

Cindy opens the bathroom door a crack and says, "Here are my clothes. Don't open the door."

"Don't worry darling. I wouldn't think of it. Here is the outfit I want you to change into after you clean yourself up."

―――――――

Cindy washes and realizes the only part of the outfit given to her is a blouse and skirt. She opens the bathroom door a crack to see if the clown is still in the room. After seeing she is alone in the room, she runs over to the dresser to find panties and some kind of bra, because her momma says she needs to start wearing a support for her developing breasts. She opens the dresser drawer and can find no underwear. She is sure there was underwear in the drawers when she first looked into them. She quickly puts on the blouse and slips the skirt up to her hips.

The door to the bedroom opens and the clown brings in a tray of food for dinner.

―――――――

"You look beautiful, darling."

"Where is the underwear? There was underwear in the drawer. I need panties and a bra," says Cindy.

"Honey, I realized I had purchased the wrong size. I will need to get you some tomorrow."

"I don't like it I don't have underwear. Where are my clothes? I have underwear."

"They are still in the washing machine. Now, look what I have brought you. I didn't know what you liked, so I brought several types of food for your dinner."

"I don't want any dinner. I want to go home. When is this party?"

"The rest of the kids haven't arrived yet. The party can't start until they get here."

"What kids? Where are they?"

"They will be here shortly. Now, when you finish your dinner, leave the tray at the door and I will come and get it later. You should get some sleep. You look tired and it has been a long day."

"What do I sleep in?" asks Cindy.

"Whatever you like."

NIGHTMARE AT NIGHT

Cindy finds something to eat and is beginning to feel sleepy. She cannot find any pajamas to wear so she decides to keep on the blouse and skirt and buries herself under the covers of the bed. She pulls the quilt up tight under her neck and tries to keep her eyes open. It isn't long before she loses the battle and her eyes close and a deep sleep follows.

Cindy begins to dream she is back home in her own bed, but something in her dream doesn't seem right. She sees a faint dark figure walking towards her bed. Suddenly, she feels cold as if the bed coverings were no longer covering her. The dark figure is rubbing her hair and forehead. "Oh, it must be daddy. He always likes to massage my head before I go to sleep," she continues to dream.

"Daddy, I love you."

"Daddy loves you, too, darling."

"Daddy, can you help me put on my pajamas? I am cold. Mommy tucked me into bed without my pajamas."

Cindy waits for her daddy to get her pajamas and wonders why he is kissing her on her lips.

"He has never done that before. He always kisses me on my forehead or cheek and he has never touched my chest. Why is he touching my bumps on my chest?" Cindy continues to dream as she shifts her body.

"Something isn't right. It feels weird down there. Daddy, mommy told me to never let anyone touch me down there." Cindy whimpers and shifts her body while pressing her legs tightly together. She sees the dark figure move farther away from her bed. Her bedroom door opens and then closes.

Cindy wakes from a restless night of sleep and sees sunshine flowing through the small windows in the basement room. She wonders why the bed covers are no longer covering her and her blouse is unbuttoned. The bumps on her chest are red in color and feel sore. On further exploration, Cindy feels embarrassed that she peed the bed.

"Why is it so wet down there? Oh, I have never had pee that was slippery. It is all over me down there, and on my legs, and I am sore down there, too."

BREAKFAST

J udd Finney is on his way down the basement stairs to give
Cindy her breakfast.

"Good morning darling," says Judd Finney.

"I have brought you breakfast. I hope you like eggs and pancakes."

"I don't want any breakfast!"

"You have to eat. I don't want you to think a clown is starving you."

"I want to go home now."

"I will clean your bed for you while you wash up."

"How do you know I messed up the bed?"

"It appears you peed the bed. I see it running down your legs."

"It is not pee. It is something else!"

"Look, I have to go to the park today. I promised the kids I would
show them a new trick today. I expect you will be a good girl and not
make trouble while I am gone. I brought you some books to read.
When I get back, we will have the party."

"You said we were having the party yesterday. I don't believe there
is going to be a party and I don't think you are a clown."

"Why do you say that, darling?"

"Clowns don't trap kids and take them from their homes."

"After I get back from the park, and the other kids get here, we will have the party and I promise I will return you to your home."

ANOTHER ONE MISSING

The phone rings at Betsy's desk and the woman on the other end of the phone asks to speak with Julia.

"Hello, this is Chief Lillus. What can I do for you?"

"My name is Thelma Baker and my daughter is missing. She went to the park this morning and hasn't returned home. It isn't like her to not come home."

"Did she go alone, to the park?" asks Julia.

"Yes, she went to the park to see the clown with the other kids. He was going to show the children some new tricks and my daughter wanted to see them too."

"How old is your daughter, Mrs. Baker?"

"My daughter, Kaitlin, is fourteen years old and has long black hair. She has dark skin and is wearing jeans with a green sweater."

"What time did she go to the park?"

"It was around nine this morning. About the time the clown shows up at the park."

"Mrs. Baker, we will patrol the park and ask questions. Sit tight, your daughter might have stopped by some of her friends before deciding to go back to your home. I will be touch with you when I get more information."

"Thank you, Chief Lillus. Please find my daughter!"

Julia enters into Bobbie's office and waits until she is finished with her phone call.

"Julia, I just got off the phone with a lady who says her daughter is missing."

"I am here to tell you I just got off the phone with a woman who says her daughter is missing too."

"Is there any progress in finding Cindy Myers?" asks Bobbie.

"No, there is no trace of her. I am concerned. We now have three girls missing; young teenagers and preteens. Each one of them went to the park and now they are missing."

"Julia, I am feeling that we have a pattern here."

What, besides the girls missing from the park, is there to the pattern?" asks Julia.

"The only thing I can think of is the clown; Mr. Judd Finney. He has been at the park every day this week."

"Bobbie, do you suspect?"

"It is possible."

"Ask Richard to get over to the records office and run a thorough check on pedophiles and rapists outside the district. Tell him to check the state records as well. I am looking for anything that might show up involving Mr. Judd Finney. Amanda, I want you to go over to the park and keep an eye on the clown. If he goes over to the ice cream shop for anything to drink, get the cup he is drinking from and run a DNA test on the saliva," says Julia.

"OK Julia, I will get a sample if it takes me all day," says Amanda.

THE PARTY IS STARTING

J udd Finney starts home from the park and arrives at his home a
half hour later. Cindy hears him arrive and unlock the door to
the basement room.

"Hey, honey, the party is about to begin!"

"These three sweethearts are going to join you at the party. Now,
you be the big girl and show them how to get cleaned up and changed
into some clean clothes. More outfits are in the dresser drawer. Oh, I
did not get a chance to go to the store for panties and a bra. You will
have to go without them for now."

"Hey, girls, you listen to Cindy. She will fill you in on how to get
ready for the party. The party starts in two hours, so be sure to be
ready," says Judd Finney.

"What party?" the two girls ask in unison.

"There is't going to be a party. He is just saying that. He has
kidnapped us," says Cindy

JUDD FINNEY LEAVES THE ROOM WHILE CINDY TALKS TO THE THREE GIRLS

"Who are you?" asks one of the girls.

"My name is Cindy and I have been here for a couple of days. I was lured here by him, the clown, with his puppies."

"Yeah, we were too."

"What is he going to do with us and what is the party?"

"He hasn't done anything yet and I do not know what the party is. I do not think there is a party," says Cindy.

"Have you had to sleep here?"

"Yes, and we have to wear these 'outfits' with no underwear," says Cindy.

"What? No underwear? Why?"

"He claims he hasn't the right size, but there was some here when I first arrived. I think he took them on purpose."

"What about the outfit? The blouse looks pretty sleazy and the skirt is a bit short, isn't it?"

"Yes, I agree, but it is all we have to wear and without underwear, well, we don't want to be around him with no clothes on," says Cindy.

"By the way, my name is Claire."

"My name is Mary."

"My name is Kaitlin. He just grabbed me and locked me in his van. I have to have underwear; I am having my period.," says Kaitlin.

"I read somewhere this guy would kidnap young girls and he would keep them for a very long time. It said that this guy was touching them in their private areas," says Mary.

"Oh, I hope not! I could get pregnant. My mom says I can get pregnant now I have my period," says Kaitlin.

"We are not going to be here long. He isn't going to be touching me. We have to find a way out of here," says Claire.

"Well, we are not going to think what he might do to us. Let's plan our escape for tonight," says Mary.

"What are your thoughts?" asks Cindy.

"We wait until he goes to the park tomorrow and we will devise a way to get out of one of those windows up there. We can break the glass and we can lift each other to get to the window and then we can pull the last one of us with a 'rope' made of a rolled-up bed sheet," says Claire.

"Sounds like a good plan to me. What are we going to do about the party tonight? Suppose it has something to do with him touching us?" asks Mary.

"No matter what, we won't let that happen. Between the four of us, we can somehow overpower him if needed. We need to keep him busy getting stuff for us and at least one of us will keep an eye open through the night in case he tries something. We can take shifts on staying awake and watching," says Cindy.

"OK, girls, I hope you are ready, because the party is about to begin," says Judd on the other side of the basement room door.

He opens the door all decked out in his clown suit; has a big cake with sparkler type candles; balloons; and the puppies who are more than happy to see the girls.

"I made the cake and punch myself. Which one of you wants me to make a balloon animal?"

"No Mr. Clown, you have forgotten the plates and cups," says Kaitlin.

"Oh, how forgetful of me, I will be right back. By the way, you darlings look stunning in those outfits."

"He makes me sick," says Mary under her breath.

"OK, here are the plates and the cups. I even remembered the napkins. Let's turn on some lullabies, shall we?"

"What are we going to do at this party?" asks Cindy.

"We are going to eat, first, and then I am going to play a game with you and demonstrate a few tricks. Just like I do at the park, except this is a private party."

In order to not get the clown angry, the four girls take part in eating a piece of cake and drinking the punch. Judd, the clown, shows the girls some tricks and gets them involved with a guessing game. The girls hate it but play along just to get him out of the room, so they can get some rest.

"Mr. Clown, can we end this party? I am getting really sleepy," says Mary.

"Me too says," Cindy.

"Aw, c'mon my darlings, the party has just started," says the clown.

Judd waits as one by one each girl falls asleep.

"Wonderful punch, huh sweeties? Notice I didn't have any," says Judd.

Judd carefully picks up each girl and lays them down on the bed. He slowly takes his clown suit off and takes a shower. He returns to the room where the four girls lay asleep and removes his trousers and then his underwear. He takes the tube of lubricant from the dresser drawer......

THE MORNING AFTER

The girls start to wake from their deep sleep from last night.

"Oh, what was in that punch or cake? I slept like I have never done before. Oh, I can hardly walk. Why do I hurt so much?" asks Cindy.

"Me too. Oh, my, I have bruises on my inner thighs!" exclaims Claire.

"Look, we all do, and I hurt down there," says Mary.

"This stuff down there and on my legs, is the same as what was on my legs when I thought I peed the bed the other night," says Cindy.

"Look over there on the dresser. What is that tube?" asks Mary.

"It has a label which says, 'vaginal' lubricant," says Cindy.

"Oh, I know what that is. My mother has tubes of it on her bed stand. I think she uses it so she isn't hurting down there when......," says Claire.

All three girls start to tear up and start crying as each of them more thoroughly examine themselves and realize the lubricant is on and inside 'down there'.

"He did something to us 'down there'! I think they call it rape!" blurts Mary.

"Oh! I am afraid I am pregnant. What should I to do?" asks Kaitlin.

"We need to get out of here now!" says Claire.

"Has he left for the park yet?" asks Cindy.

"It is ten in the morning. If he is going to the park, he has already left. I am not waiting. I am leaving now!" exclaims Mary.

"Quick, hoist me up to the window, but first, give me that lamp base. I need something to break the window," says Claire.

The girls manage to break the window and remove as much glass as possible before shimmying the way out of it. Mary rolls up the bedsheet tightly to make a 'rope' and pulls Cindy, the last girl, up and through the window.

"How do we get back to our homes?" asks Cindy.

"Where are we, anyway?" asks Claire.

"Wait, let's see if we can get someone out on the street to stop and call our parents to come and get us," suggests Kaitlin.

RAPED BY A CLOWN

The girls run out to the street and manage to get a motorist to
stop and call their parents.

"Chief Lillus, Ellie Myers just called and said Cindy called her and
asked to be brought home. The other three missing girls are with
Cindy. Something about being locked in the basement of a home,"
says Betsy.

"Did they say where they were being kept captive?"

"No, Chief Lillus, they did not. Oh, they are here. The four girls
and their mothers."

"Show them in right away, Betsy."

"Girls, what can you tell me about your abduction?" asks Julia.

"We were taken captive by the clown and he took us to a room and
kept us there," says Cindy.

"Did he do anything to you? Did he touch you inappropriately?"

"We are not sure. He had a 'party' for us last night and we fell
asleep. This morning when we awakened we noticed we were sore
and had some kind of lubricant 'down there'," says Mary.

"'Down there'? Do you mean your private parts; your vagina?" asks Julia.

"Yes," responded all four girls simultaneously.

"Chief Lillus, I am afraid he made me pregnant!" exclaims Kaitlin.

"Ladies, you need to take your girls to the hospital emergency room right away! There needs to be tests for penetration, STD's and a chance for…you know where I am going with this," says Julia.

"My girl hasn't had her period yet."

"Neither has mine."

"Mine has," says Mrs. Baker.

"It does not matter. Get them to the hospital now!" exclaims Julia.

The mothers and daughters heed Julia's orders and rush off to the emergency room.

"Amanda, please follow them to the emergency room. Here, take this official release with you to get samples of the vaginal fluids of each of the girls. Were you able to get a DNA sample of Judd Finney?" asks Julia.

"Oh, yes, I got his DNA. If he penetrated and/or released semen, I will have proof that Mr. Finney raped those young girls while they were being held captive," says Amanda.

"Richard, take Bobbie and get over to the park. Bring the clown in here for questioning," says Julia.

QUESTIONING A CLOWN

R ichard and Bobby find the clown at the park and take him to
Julia for questioning.

"Mr. Finney, I assume you have had your rights read to you by my
Deputies?" asks Julia.

"Yes, I have. I do not know why you have brought me here. You
have ruined my reputation with the children by hauling me out of the
park by your Deputies."

"Mr. Finney, my understanding is you have four young ladies
under the age of sixteen locked in your home in a basement room?"

"The young ladies you are referring were over to my home for a
party. I sometimes invite children over to give them a party."

"Are the young ladies at your home at this time?"

"No, absolutely not! I took them home after the party way before
dark, and they came to my party voluntarily, in case you are
wondering."

"Mr. Finney, do you feel it wise to bring or invite young underage
ladies to your home without adult supervision, such as their parents?

And, do you expect me to believe that these young ladies would just come over to a man's home alone, who they do not know?"

"Why not, I am a clown and children can always trust a clown. Besides, these young ladies you are referring to are safe back at home I am sure, unharmed."

"Mr. Judd Finney, I am arresting you for the abduction of underage children, against their will, with the intent to harm them in a sexual manner," says Julia.

"Chief, you have gotten it all wrong! I haven't touched those girls and they are safe at home!" exclaims Judd Finney.

"Lock him up Richard!"

THE FORENSICS LAB

T he new Forensics Lab is already become an important asset to the Harford Police Department.

"Amanda, did you have any trouble with getting the vaginal fluid samples?" asks Julia.

"No, not at all, there is a lot of lubricant mixed in and there does not appear to be any semen found at this time, but something or someone penetrated each of those girls."

"Well, there was a lapse of time since the act was supposedly done and the time the samples were taken. Any semen would have run out of them in that amount of time. Being the girls as young as they are, probably wouldn't have realized any semen discharge," says Julia.

"You are right Julia. Those girls were virgins at the time."

"Will semen remnants show up in the fluid after a so-called discharge?" asks Julia.

"Yes, I believe so. The stuff is a bit sticky. I would assume some remnants would still be within the fluid."

"Amanda, were you ever married?" asks Julia.

"Well, no, and I know what you are getting at. I definitely do not have any reason to know such things, but my Forensic Studies has taught me quite a bit about semen and its properties."

"You are blushing, Amanda. Please get to me your results when you are through. I like having a Forensics Lab right here in the Department."

"Right, Julia. It should only take about an hour. I will test each girl's fluid independently to see if semen was introduced during penetration."

JULIA IS WAITING TO HEAR FROM THE MOTHERS OF THE THREE GIRLS WITH THE FINDINGS FROM THE EMERGENCY ROOM. SHE ALSO IS ANTICIPATING AMANDA'S RESULTS.

"Julia, I have the results from the tests. The DNA taken from the glass Mr. Finney drank from and the vaginal fluids of the three girls is a direct match. We are lucky, I almost did not have a trace of DNA with one of the girls' sample. From my findings, I have determined that Mr. Finney first penetrated the older girl, Kaitlin, releasing his semen, and then while still able or at a later time, penetrated the second girl and then the third girl. He only ejaculated once, but the trace from one girl to the next got weaker, meaning he dragged some of his semen each time he penetrated. I also found he was, at the time, taking the erectile dysfunction drug, thus being able to penetrate the other two girls after his ejaculation."

"Wow more than I care to listen to, but thanks, Amanda."

THE CLOWN AND THE VERDICT

M r. Judd Finney has his day in court.

"Please rise. The court of the State vs. Mr. Judd Finney is now in session. The Honorable Judge Horton is residing," says the bailiff.

"Mr. Finney, you have told the court, four young ladies, who were at your home for a party, asked for you to engage in sexual relations with you. Do you understand the four ladies are under the age of sixteen and therefore, minors? Do you also understand those young ladies' tests showed that they were drugged by the 'Date Rape' drug and that particular drug was found in your home? It doesn't sound to me that they wanted to engage in sexual relations with you. You lured four young ladies into a van, portraying as a clown, and took them to a locked room in your basement and proceeded to rape them against their will with the use of a drug. The court has found you guilty of kidnapping, abduction and the rape of four young female minors. I will not allow your plea of temporary insanity, although I do believe you need mental help. I hereby sentence you to 25 years in the

Jackson City Prison and fine you with twenty-five thousand dollars to be paid to each of the four young ladies in a trust. This money is to come out of your investments and be paid in less than a month. Court is dismissed," says the Honorable Judge Horton.

"All rise," says the bailiff.

AFTERTHOUGHTS

A fter the court ruling, Julia invites the mothers of the girls to her office for conversation.

"Ladies, I have called you to my office to bring closure to your daughter's cases. I would first like to ask how your daughters are doing?"

"I think we all agree our daughters are doing well and do not seem to be affected. One good thing about the 'Date Rape' drug, in our case, is our girls didn't have to endure the act consciously and they don't understand the act of sex all that much."

"Yes, ladies, but you will need to get them into counseling. It happened to them and they will remember something sometime," says Julia.

"The hospital said that none of our daughters were infected with STDs and my Kaitlin isn't pregnant. Thank you, Chief Lillus, for all you have done."

"Well, I really didn't do too much. Your daughters did all of the work."

"We are very fortunate to have you being the Chief of Police and your Department of Deputies. Give a special thanks to Amanda."

"Yes, she is a great asset to our Department. We now have an in-house Forensics Lab," says Julia.

The ladies leave, and Richard, Bobbie and Julia are alone once again to talk over the recent case.

"Julia, you were right, again. You had concerns about that clown coming to our town," says Bobbie.

"Bobbie, as soon as I saw him, I had ill feelings about him. It isn't natural to have a clown just show up," says Julia.

"Julia, are you trying to say you have something against clowns?" asks Richard.

"No not at all Richard, clowns are, how should I say it; I kind of feel clowns are a little scary and creepy."

"Yeah, but Julia Ann liked him," says Bobbie.

"That really scares me. Julia Ann could have been a victim of that pedophile. He looked into that little girl's eyes. It was so creepy and scary," says Julia.

"At least he is apprehended early before it got any worse. I do feel sorry for those four young girls, though. Do you think we will ever get out from under these strange cases?" asks Richard.

"I am not sure, Richard, I am not sure," says Julia.

"Hey Julia, Richard and I do have some good news for you."

"No, Bobbie, don't tell me. Are you pregnant again?"

"Yup, we are!"

"Oh my God, you two…."

"I guess I am going to have to split you two up more often on these cases we get. Too much 'hanky-panky' going on!"

"Oh, Julia, you are too funny! Just too funny!" exclaims Bobbie.

EPILOGUE

O nce again, the Harford Police Department has endured a couple of strange cases.

Julia is much more confident in solving the cases at a faster pace with the addition of the new Forensics Lab and Amanda Alexandria.

Richard and Bobbie never cease to amaze Julia in how much zest they have for each other and is assured she will have a passel of Peltz children to keep her mind busy while fulfilling a need she was not able to have, in birthing a child.

The days role on in Harford and, today, the community is quiet.…

ABOUT THE AUTHOR

James Roberts is an emerging author of Murder, Erotic Sex, Rape, and Deceit.

The reader is challenged by the experiences seen through the eyes of his characters, and although fiction in nature, allows the reader to experience real-life situations relatable to their world, and invites the reader to explore their inner feelings of right and wrong based on those experiences.

This is Book Three of A Julia Lillus Series of adult books written by James Roberts.